The Proud Rebel

When the remnants of the Confederate Army, broken and defeated, made their way slowly south from the battle fields, Dave Kelsey turned his eyes towards Virginia, to the home he had left four long years before. But all his plans were cast aside when he found the ranch-house a burnt-out shell and all his family dead, killed by men more deadly than just the ragged and battle-hungry Union soldiers. Men just as eager to kill him in turn.

They sent men with guns after him, branded him a traitor and an outlaw, and put the law to hunt him down. But this proved to be a costly mistake, for soon there was nowhere else for Kelsey to run, so he came back at them, a lone gun, a man on a mission of revenge who knew he could stay alive only by his skill with a Colt.

The town, the range and the law all belonged to the men who were trying to kill him, so he made his own law with a .45.

The Proud Rebel

Michael Stansfield

A Black Horse Western

ROBERT HALE · LONDON

© 1967, 2002 John Glasby
First hardcover edition 2002
Originally published in paperback as
The Wild Gun by Chuck Adams

ISBN 0 7090 7221 X

Robert Hale Limited
Clerkenwell House
Clerkenwell Green
London EC1R 0HT

Typeset by
Derek Doyle & Associates, Liverpool.
Printed and bound in Great Britain by
Antony Rowe Limited, Wiltshire

1

The Proud Rebel

Clayton was a typical North Virginia town, loose and
rambling, with the wooden buildings strewn about the
main street and along the bank of the river that wound
sluggishly through the heavily wooded countryside to the
north. It was as if the stores, hotels and houses had simply
been thrown up haphazardly without any regard at all to
order. When Dave Kelsey had ridden through it almost
four years before, riding north to join the Confederate
Army, it had been only half of its present size and, in spite
of it having been captured by the Union forces less than a
year after the outbreak of war, retaken by the
Confederates eighteen months later, purged and
garrisoned by both sides in turn during the last two years
of conflict when an entire nation had trembled on the
brink of ruin, it had grown considerably.

Here and there patches of blackened rubble had still
not been cleared away, remained as battle scars to show
that it had, more than once, been in the front line of the
war. Even the newer buildings that clustered near the railroad were of pine and maple, only the fresh cut of the
timber marking them out from the others. The builders
had not worried overmuch about decoration, had simply

taken the materials which abounded naturally in the area so that the structures were not really built to last but blended in with their surroundings.

Dave was cold and hungry, and shivered a little in the chill northerly wind that blew the grey dust off the main street into his eyes and nostrils. He fingered the handful of coins in his mackinaw pocket, checked his mount halfway along the street and stared with hooded eyes about him. Night had come to Clayton and already there were rows of yellow lights cutting through the gloom on the boardwalk. He noticed there were plenty of blue uniforms in the street and, for a moment, the feeling of defeat and heartbreak came back to him at the sight of the arrogant men who strode the boardwalks as though they owned the place.

He had been little more than a runt-sized kid when he had gone to the wars – but in the four years since then he had become a man, broad-shouldered, narrow-waisted, eyes that stared out at the world with a look that betrayed nothing. He had learned many things in the white heat of battle, things a man is forced to learn in war, was well able to stay alive, knowing it now to be a cruel and often merciless business.

Gigging his mount softly, he walked it along the street. Music drifted on the cold night wind from the lighted windows of the saloons, music and raucous laughter, the shouts of men. Clayton had grown and it had changed, too. There seemed to be plenty of money circulating but he noticed that it was mostly the influx of Northerners who had it to spend; the fat-bellied business men who had come south to bleed the Southern States white, the carpet-baggers and those Virginians who preferred the hard yellow gold to any pride in their State.

Dave tethered his mount to a lop-sided wooden rail where a broken wall, angling away from a low-roofed shack, took some of the icy bite from the wind. Easing the cinch, he stepped up on to the boardwalk, deadening echoes in the creaking wooden boards. Then he eased his way into the lamplit glare of the saloon. A score of lamps hung from the rafters stretched width-way across the room. Finding himself a place at the bar, he ordered whisky, drank it slowly, letting his gaze wander over the faces of the men around him. He did not expect to see any he recognised. Four years had changed things far too much; four years and the war that had stretched in between. War as it had been fought on the northern borders of Virginia. The charge at dawn through a writhing fog of mist and gunsmoke, the quick skirmish in the night, the shrieking yells of wounded and dying men around him, the glint of moonlight off naked bayonets, the bark and whine of the Sharp's rifle and the long days and nights in the wilderness when they fought against tremendous odds to half the Army of the North.

War. It was over now. The skulking in the undergrowth, the sniping, flight and pursuit, the burning buildings put to the torch, his companions dying in the muck and green slime, pillars of smoke climbing high over doomed towns, their streets running with the blood of the slain. No quarter asked for, and none given by either side – and towards the end, when it became increasingly obvious that everything was lost, the guerilla warfare, the small bands of men, striking fast and hard in the night and then melting back into the shadows.

The bitterness came back to his face as he poured himself his second drink, felt the raw liquor burn the back of his throat on the way down. They had fought a war and they had lost; and now they were having to pay for it. The signing of the treaty at Appomattox was some months back and Dave Kelsey was only just on his way back home.

Finishing his drink, he moved over to one of the tables where a poker game was in progress, stood on the fringe of the group of men clustered around the players. It didn't take Dave ten minutes to spot that the game was crooked. A thin man dressed in gambler's clothes was holding the cards, dealing them swiftly with his left hand. Frenchy LaVere, out from Mississippi and New Orleans, wanted for a score of murders along the river, a fast gunman with a reputation that was as sharp as the rest of his features. He flicked the cards across the table to the other three men, fanned his own hand in front of him with a professional twist of his forefinger and thumb. As an onlooker, Dave had plenty of chance to study the other men and it did not take him long to realise that two of them, broad, beefy men, were in league with LaVere, the three of them lined up against the fourth man, who sat hunched forward with his elbows on the table, puffing hard on his cigar. He was short and slender, with the dark skin and crinkly black hair that spoke of Mexican blood.

The Mexican was not a good poker player and Dave wondered how often he had played with these men. He pushed his hands much too hard even when they were mediocre, scowled viciously whenever he lost and one of the other three took the pot. Evidently they had let him win the first few hands and were now taking back what he had won and much more besides.

When he was certain how the men were operating, he decided to take a hand himself, stepped forward, brushing past the man who stood beside him. Out of the corner of his eye, he saw the other glance up quickly at his movement and softly, speaking out of the corner of is mouth, the man said: 'It's a real rough country here, friend. I figure this is none of your business.'

The words were clearly meant as a friendly warning, but Dave gave a curt nod. 'I'll be best judge of that,' he said quietly. He moved around the table to where an empty chair stood a little way from the Mexican.

'Mind if I take a hand?' he inquired, glancing across at the thin-faced gambler.

Frenchy LaVere lifted his glance. For a long moment the cold, empty gaze stared through Dave, almost as if he were not there. Then the other inclined his head briefly.

'Sit in if you wish, my friend,' he said, smiling thinly, showing a flash of even white teeth. 'But the stakes are inclined to be high.' There was a slightly insolent note to his tone as his gaze lowered itself from Dave's face and passed over his clothing.

'That's all right by me.' He felt inside his belt, drew out some of the gold coins there and stacked them on the table in front of him, pretending not to notice the sudden glitter in the eyes of the three men facing him across the table.

As the hand was dealt the men seemed open and friendly. Only the Mexican regarded him curiously and with a faint distrust on his features. But in spite of the outward friendliness, Dave knew that they were assessing him, trying to figure out who he was, and especially where he had got the money. Judging from the character of the men and from the little he had heard of Frenchy LaVere, he guessed that if they failed to clean him out by cheating at cards, they would soon find other means of doing it, in one of the narrow back alleys of the town; the butt of a Colt on the back of the skull, perhaps, or even a bullet in the back.

He deliberately played the first few hands dealt him cautiously and poorly. They cost him very little in real money and, as he felt the tension relax a little, he was able to concentrate on studying the cards. As he had figured, the cards were all marked, not too skilfully, but evidently sufficiently so for the Mexican not to have noticed.

Frenchy tapped his fingers on top of the table. He was staring straight at Dave. Pursing his lips, Dave eyed the cards once more, then tossed them on to the table. 'I'm out,' he said, sitting back in his chair.

LaVere nodded almost imperceptibly, then did a strange thing. Before moving on to the Mexican on Dave's left, he gave a quick signal to the bartender. The other caught the gesture, nodded, brought over a bottle and a glass and set them down beside Dave's right hand.

'You look as though you've travelled a long way,' said

Frenchy. 'Get some of the trail dust out of your throat before the next hand.'

The Mexican flashed Frenchy an annoyed glance, but said nothing, drumming with his fingertips on the table as he waited for two cards to cover those he had just thrown in.

'Let's get on with the game, *amigo*,' he snapped. 'I didn't come here to wait while you bought drinks for every stranger in Clayton.'

LaVere smiled, a cold twitching of his lips. 'All in good time, Marengo. You still have most of the night left to win back your money.'

Marengo frowned at that remark, opened his mouth to say something further, and then decided against it. He sank back into his chair, picked up the two cards which the other flicked in his direction, lifted them one at a time, his face expressionless at first, then showing a sudden gleam of excitement. Dave reckoned that he had been deliberately dealt a seemingly unbeatable hand in order for him to bet it to the limit. Glancing at the other three men over the rim of his glass, he caught the glance which passed among them, knew they had set up the Mexican for their first big kill of the evening. Once he lost a pile on this hand, he would be hooked for the rest of the evening, forced to play on in the hope of recouping his heavy losses and, with each hand they played, he would merely sink deeper and deeper into their trap.

First one of LaVere's cronies threw in his hand and then the other, leaving only Marengo and the gambler in the game.

By now the Mexican's face was flushed with excitement, and the hesitation with which Frenchy pushed a stack of coins forward into the middle of the table to join the others gave him added confidence that his was the better hand.

Finally LaVere said softly: 'Very well, *mon ami*, I call. What have you got?'

With a look of triumph, Marengo fanned his cards in

front of him. 'Eights,' he said. 'All four of them.' He reached for the pot, his hands crooked in front of him.

'Not so fast,' interrupted Frenchy LaVere. Slowly he faced his own cards. 'Four jacks.'

Marengo stared open-mouthed at the cards. His hands were twitching, his face white.

Grinning, Frenchy gathered the pot towards him, stacked it neatly in front of him. 'Better luck on the next hand,' he said lightly. 'Your luck is sure to turn before the evening is out.'

The Mexican's face was livid now. Sucking in a sharp breath, he let it go in a harsh hiss. 'Goddamn luck,' he snarled viciously. 'Seems to me that—'

'That what, *mon ami*?' Frenchy eyes him intently from beneath lowered lids.

'Nothing,' muttered the other after a brief pause.

'Let's get on with the game and stop the talk,' growled the pudgy-faced man on Dave's right. He chinked some coins from one hand to the other. For the next half-dozen hands very little money moved across the table. The pots were small and Marengo won two of them, but this did little to sweeten his temper.

How was it that the other had not yet tumbled to the fact that he was being cheated? Dave wondered. Frenchy shuffled the cards, placed the pack in the centre of the table. 'Cut,' he said to Marengo.

Dave decided that now was the time to act. Stretching out his hand before the Mexican could make a move, he drew the pack towards him, said quietly:

'Perhaps there is no need to cut the cards.' Still keeping his glance on Frenchy LaVere, his left hand hidden below the level of the table, he picked off the top card and, without turning it over, merely feeling the marks which had been made around the edge, he said: 'Ace of Clubs.' He flicked it over almost contemptuously, went on: 'Six of Hearts; ten of Diamonds; king of Spades.'

As the cards fell face upwards on the table, he flashed

an amused grin at the three men opposite him, saw the narrowing of Frenchy LaVere's eyes, the uncertainty on the faces of his two companions, the dawning apprehension on Marengo's swarthy features, the growing certainty that appeared in the dark eyes.

Then, with a sudden, lithe movement, LaVere was on his feet, backed away a couple of paces from the table. His right hand was close to the gun in the holster at his waist, holding the black frock coat back with his wrist. His lips twisted themselves into a vicious grin. 'That was not a wise thing to do, *mon ami*,' he said very softly. 'Nobody does that to French LaVere and lives.'

'They were cheating me,' breathed Marengo. 'For that I will kill them.' He made to push back his chair and get to his feet, his features suffused with rage. His voice shook a little, but there was enough anger in him to send him lunging forward in spite of the menace of Frenchy's gun.

'Better sit down,' Dave said sharply. 'This is now between Frenchy and me. I don't like crooked gamblers any more than you do. They're the vultures who move in after the kill.' As he spoke, he kept his gaze locked with the other's, saw the momentary hesitation on the man's face. Frenchy LaVere was not quite sure of himself now. He edged his hand a little closer to the butt of the gun protruding from the holster.

'Try for that and you're a dead man,' Dave said quietly.

Frenchy sneered. 'You must be a bigger fool than I thought,' he said derisively. 'I can draw and shoot you before you can make a move for your gun. By sitting there, you've signed your death warrant.'

Dave shook his head slowly. 'You've got it all wrong, Frenchy. There's a .45 pointed at your belly beneath this table right now with my finger on the trigger. The first move you make, you'll get a slug in your stomach. Now why don't you just turn around and get out of here, and take your two friends with you.'

Frenchy hesitated at that, face changing colour. For a

moment his gaze lowered to the table in front of him, as if he were trying to stare through the solid wood and see whether or not Dave was bluffing. His tongue flicked out and wet the thinly stretched lips.

'You're bluffing,' he said after a long pause.

'Am I? Then why don't you put in your chips and find out? Now either take your hand away from that gun and get out, or make your play.'

Frenchy stood and hesitated. There was the feel of eyes on him, urging him to action. He knew he had either to risk Dave bluffing him, or back down in front of all of these men, and the knowledge was as gall in his mouth. But eventually caution triumphed in his mind. Whatever else he was, Frenchy was no fool. He had killed many men in his career along the Mississippi river, most of them shot before they could make a move towards their weapons, or too drunk to be able to handle them even if they had the chance. But this man was different. The cold, enigmatic eyes that bored into his own told him nothing other than that he would do exactly as he said and shoot him down if he made any move. He felt a cold chill inside the room which had, only a few moments before, been warm, and its touch was like the icy fingers of death ruffling the small hairs on the back of his neck.

It was the man on Frenchy's left who broke the intolerable tension in the saloon as he let a small sigh escape from his lips, an exhalation that betrayed him.

Slowly Frenchy moved his hand away from the gun, let the frock coat fall back into place. He was still quivering with a cold rage and some of it showed through in his tone as he said thinly: 'You haven't heard the last of this, *mon ami*. I shall remember your face until the trump of doom. Wherever you are I shall come after you. This is only the beginning as far as you and I are concerned, not the end.'

'If that's the way you want it, Frenchy, that's the way it's going to be.' He remained seated at the table, his left hand placed in front of him as the three men turned in unison and walked out of the saloon, the batwing doors swinging shut at their backs.

Dave looked for a moment at the empty doorway, then let a small sigh of relief come from his lips. Slowly he brought his right hand into view from beneath the table. It was empty. He noticed the look of incredulous surprise on the Mexican's face as the other stared down at him. It had been a taut, strained moment when tension had crackled in the room and the slightest wrong movement could have started guns roaring. He ran a dry tongue over equally dry lips and reached for the whisky bottle, pouring the amber liquid into the empty glass..

'Amigo,' said Marengo, his face still surprised, 'you are either a fool or a very brave man. I am not certain which. That man is a killer. I have heard stories of him.'

Dave's face was hard. 'They're all the same. They'll kill a man when they know they have the edge on him, just as they have to have an edge to take his money from him at poker. Make them uncertain as to the pay and they back down.'

He got to his feet, took a handful of coins from the pile on the table in front of the empty chair which Frenchy had occupied. 'I guess this covers my losses for the evening. Reckon the rest will cover you for what they must have cheated you out of.'

The other hesitated, then scooped up the coins, thrust them into his pockets. 'I would have killed them, all three,' he said at length. 'Perhaps I still will.'

'You've got the money, why look for more trouble?' Dave muttered. He moved away towards the bar, carrying the half-empty bottle with him, setting it down in front of the bartender. 'Any place around here where a man can get a bed for the night?'

Marengo came up beside him. 'I am greatly in your debt, Senor. You will have a room at the hotel where I am staying. Please.' He held up his hand as Dave made to argue. 'I will hear no more.'

'You owe me nothing,' Dave said.

'If you say so.' The other shrugged. His tone dropped a little. 'But I can judge a lot from a man's appearance. I can see what you are. The war is over, but not for you. This town is changed. A man in your position is watched and not only Frenchy and his friends will be on the look out for you. You need the help of someone who knows and understands this town.'

There was no moon as the two men left the saloon and stepped down into the street, and dark clouds, scudding in front of the wind, blotted out the stars. Untethering the horse, Dave walked beside Marengo. He was, by habit, a quick-moving, restless man and he chafed a little at the slow walk of the Mexican.

Leaving the horse at the livery stables, Dave stepped towards the entrance, halted as Marengo laid a restraining hand on his arm.

'Careful, amigo. I thought I saw something just across the street. It may have been a shadow, but I do not think so.'

An uncomfortable silence lay over the street as Dave peered into the night. He was not a man given to hesitation. Easing the Colt from its holster, he said quietly: 'Cover me from here.'

'Don't be a fool,' hissed the Mexican. 'They can shoot you down from three directions at once.'

'Maybe so. But they've got to see me first,' Dave replied. Without waiting for the other to reply, he slid sideways on bent legs, his shoulders brushing the front of the building at his back. Crouching down behind one of the wooden uprights, Don Marengo drew his own gun and waited. He heard nothing from the direction in which Dave had vanished. The man moved like a cat, he thought to himself, making no sound, no longer visible. Then, a brief moment later, he just caught a glimpse of a fleeting shadow that moved across the main street and melted into the darkness on the opposite boardwalk thirty yards from the alley.

Still crouched, Dave moved towards the alley with slow, careful steps, keeping his glance on the black opening. He was less than ten feet from it when a sound reached him, the squeaking of rusty hinges. He paused, waited for any further sound, but none came. Cautiously, a little unsure of how well Marengo could handle a gun, not wanting to be shot by the other if a showdown came, he edged towards the alley.

Halfway along the alley he noticed the looming bulk of a twin-storey grain store and, a moment later, he heard the stir of feet on straw, paused for only a moment, then threw himself around the corner of the alley, pressing himself hard against the low wall that ran back towards the store. The bottom storey was in the form of a long, low shed, the far end completely dark with nothing showing at all. A half-dozen bales of straw were just visible inside the opening and, even as he moved forward again, a gun boomed, rocking the store, an orange stiletto of flame in the darkness. The slug whined over Dave's head as he automatically dropped to his knees and he heard the splintering of wood behind him at the point where his belt would have been.

There was the rush of boots on the floor of the grain store and Dave fired into the darkness a little to the left of the point where the flash of flame had been. There came a low grunt of agony and he knew his bullet had found its mark in a man's body. The next second more gunfire broke out from the concealing shadows and lead hummed through the air all around Dave's crouching body. He reckoned that all three gunmen were holed up in the grain store, knew he had to flush them out before they managed to pin him down.

Getting his legs under him, keeping a tight grip on the Colt in his right hand, he lurched forward, running for the bales of straw. He heard the men move away, deeper into the store. A gun roared directly in front of him, the blue-crimson flash lighting the interior of the building for a brief fraction of a second. Lunging off balance, he went down, his body rolling to one side against one of the bales. He felt the air knocked from his lungs as he struck the ground, and a numbing pain jarred redly along his arm. A man came stumbling forward out of the darkness, swinging a Colt, striving to hammer at Dave's head with the upraised weapon.

Unable to use his gun at such close quarters, Dave went down with the other on top of him, squirming beneath the man as the butt of the gun caught him a glancing blow on the side of the skull. Jerking his head to one side, he rolled away, dazed by the blow, sick, coming to a stop on his stomach, the man's knee in the small of his back. Sucking a gust of air into his heaving lungs, he pushed himself up on to his arms, swung the man off with a tremendous effort.

He heard the other give a grunt of pain as he fell, the edge of one of the bales striking him just above the kidneys. Dave did not wait to give him the chance to recover but jerked forward, swinging the barrel of the revolver against the man's temple. The other sagged and collapsed as though pole-axed. Kneeling over the other, Dave saw, as he had begun to suspect, that it was one of the pudgy-faced men who had been with Frenchy LaVere. His eyes moved on to search the blackness at the rear of the store. LaVere and the other man were still there, concealed in the shadows, waiting for him to make a move.

There was a long silence and then, out of the darkness Dave heard a faint rustle, an exhalation of pent-up breath. As if the other realised he had just given away his position, a gunblast roared inside the store but the bullet went wild. Dave had his own gun steady in his hand, lined it up on the muzzle flash and loosed off a couple of shots. There was the shrill whine of ricochets, then more slugs struck the shelves just above his head, tearing splinters from the wood. Sliding sideways, he fired at a shadow that flitted along the back of the store, a shadow that leapt to one side, lunged against the wall. A moment later he heard a door handle being turned and an oblong of light showed as a door was opened. Briefly he caught a glimpse of a small shape that slid out into the alley at the rear of the building, snapped a quick shot at the man – knew instinctively that it was Frenchy LaVere – but the bullet missed and, a moment later, the door slammed shut.

Dave propped himself up on one elbow, the gun in his hand, listening carefully, knowing that the third man was still there, cornered and potentially dangerous. There was the sound of a horse being spurred away from the back of the grain store. Evidently Frenchy did not intend to hang around just to help his companion.

Dave said softly: 'Better step out, mister, with your hands lifted. You ain't goin' to get any help from LaVere now. He's made sure of savin' his own rotten hide.'

A pause, then a harsh voice said: 'No deal, Kelsey. I know your type. You wait until I move into the open and then drop me. If you want me, you'll have to come and get me.'

'All right, if that's the way you want it.' Triggering a single shot, Dave made a dive to one side, slithered several feet on his belly, thrust himself forward with a tremendous heave of his legs and wound up on the far side of the store. From his vantage point he peered into the gloom, was just able to make out the shape of the gunman where he lay on his belly behind a plank of wood some ten yards away. He could see the other's head turning swiftly from side to side as he tried to make out where he was. The man was beginning to get jumpy. Dave had him figured for a man unused to gunplay; content to act tough and big so long as he had a man such as Frenchy LaVere, with his killer's reputation, at the back of him. But now that the other had run out and left him, he was unsure of himself, afraid to move from his position for fear of getting a slug in him.

Grinning a little, Dave eased himself a little further to one side so that he was almost behind the other, then cocked back the hammer of the Colt, said harshly: 'Drop that gun friend. Now!'

The words echoed in the empty stillness of the place and, for a moment, the other made no move, then abruptly he reached his decision. Swinging sharply, he tried to bring his weapon to bear, his finger tightening frenziedly on the trigger. Dave's finger had been resting lightly against the tightness of the trigger so that he had only to flick it. The man was still turning when Dave fired the gun jumping in his hand. He saw the other jerk backward, saw the gun go spinning from the man's broken wrist. The other let out a howl of pain and fear, fell back on to the earthen floor of the store. Getting to his feet, Dave walked forward, the barrel of the Colt lowering on the other's body as he stood over him. In the dimness the man's wide-open eyes shone palely with fear. He ran the tip of his tongue across dry lips.

'All right, killer,' he grunted. 'What are you waitin' for? Shoot and get it over with.'

'On your feet,' Dave said tightly. He prodded the barrel in the small of the man's back, thrusting him towards the door. The first man still lay unconscious near the bales of straw. Dave gave him a cursory glance, then called softly into the darkness: 'Come on up, Marengo.' A few moments later the slender shape of the Mexican loomed out of the darkness in the alley.

'There's one of 'em still in there, unconscious,' Dave told him. 'Better drag him out and we'll hand these two over to the sheriff.'

'What about LaVere?'

'He got away. Sneaked out of the back, leaving his companions to fight as best they could.'

'That is the way he always works,' said Marengo. He went inside the store, reappeared dragging the unconscious man over the dirt.

Sheriff Tragott studied Dave carefully, watching him
closely as he stood in front of the long deal desk with
Marengo. His grey eyes were veiled, revealing nothing.
When he spoke, his voice was soft and quiet, but with a
note that Dave did not like, something more than suspicion in it. 'You any idea why these men should want to
bushwhack you, gentlemen?'

'Could be they didn't like the way I showed 'em up when
they were cheatin' Senor Marengo at poker,' Dave said.

'And this other man – LaVere – you know anythin'
about him?'

Dave narrowed his eyes down a little. 'Seems to me,
Sheriff,' he said tersely, 'that you ought to know more
about him than we do. He's got a bad reputation east of
here, along the Mississippi. Nobody knows how many men
he's killed and very few of them in fair fight or self-
defence.'

'Then you're claimin' he's wanted for murder?'

Dave tightened his lips. He had the impression that the
lawman was inwardly mocking him, paying very little attention to the legitimate complaint which he and Marengo
had made. He said quietly: 'If you don't know anythin'
about it, then I reckon it ain't up to us to tell you.'

Tragott took a cigar from his vest pocket, twirled it in
his fingers for a moment before placing it carefully
between his lips and lighting it. He puffed a cloud of
smoke in front of him and his voice was brittle as he went
on: 'As the representative of the law in Clayton, it's up to
me to get any information from you I think fit, Kelsey. This
is a law-abidin' town and I aim to keep it that way. From
what I've heard, LaVere and his friends have been in town
for some months now and there's been no complaint
against 'em in all of that time. Now you ride in and the
first night there's trouble. A shoot-out in the store, what
could have been big trouble in the saloon.'

'Seems to me you're coming out on the side of a killer against the law-abiding citizens.' Marengo gave the lawman a bright-sharp glance. 'I always believed the law should be impartial.'

'If you don't like the way the law is dispensed in this town, reckon it might be better if you rode on,' said Tragott acidly. For the first time his smooth, unperturbed front seemed to have cracked a little. The faint smile was gone from his face. He got heavily to his feet, came around the side of the desk.

'I already figure on doin just that, first thing tomorrow,' Dave said tautly. 'But in the meantime, don't you think these two men ought to be locked up? Reckon you could get the doctor to take a look at that *hombre*'s wrist.'

'You tryin' to tell me how to do my job?' There was menace now in the lawman's voice.

'No.' Dave shook his head, his tone still deceptively calm in spite of the fact that he was boiling with anger deep inside. 'Only if I see either of 'em around town before I ride out tomorrow, I'm likely to shoot 'em plumb dead and the same goes for Frenchy LaVere.'

For a moment a deep red flush climbed up the sheriff's broad features and there was a sharp glint in his eyes. Then he caught himself with an effort, gave a terse nod and went for his keys.

The appetising odour of frying pork and hot coffee woke Dave Kelsey the following morning. He dressed quickly, made his way down the stairs into the dining room of the hotel to find Marengo already there, seated at the table next to the window. The Mexican waved him over, flashed a friendly greeting.

'I guessed you'd be up early, *amigo*. First, breakfast, and then we ride out.'

Dave glanced at the other in surprise as he sat down opposite the man.

'I didn't know you were riding out, Don Marengo.'

The other shrugged, sipped his coffee slowly. 'I am a Mexican, *amigo*. I think it is time I went back to my own country. There are too many men in the north who seem interested only in the gold I carry. Besides, from what I hear, there is still danger for a man riding the trails south, even through Virginia. The war itself may be over, but there are still many who either do not know that, or prefer not to know. Two men riding these trails may be safe, whereas a lone man might never reach his home.'

Dave nodded. 'I understand.' He ate his breakfast ravenously when it came, washed it down with the hot coffee. It burned the back of his throat, but made him feel good, so that a kind of restlessness rode in him, a sort of urgency to get back home. He had been away far too long. Although the war was lost, the task of rebuilding the country still lay ahead of them. It was going to take the South years to regain what had been lost during those bitter years of bloodshed, and the sooner they got down to the task, the better.

The town was quiet as they left the hotel and walked to the livery stables. Not until they were mounted up and riding out did Dave glance over his shoulder and see Sheriff Tragott standing just inside the doorway of the jail-house. The lawman was watching them as they rode out of town. Then he turned his head away, spoke to the two men standing just behind him. Dave did not have to see them to know that they were the men who had supposedly been locked up as prisoners in the cells at the rear of the building. For a moment anger spilled up inside him, but he thrust it down quickly. It was only to be expected. These men were citizens of Clayton. Tragott would take their part against any stranger, particularly one causing trouble.

2

The Lawless Guns

The two riders checked their mounts on a broad rise of ground that looked out over the rolling lands which led south to the Kanawha river and over to the great heights of the Appalachians. Tired men who had ridden far and fast. Swaying in his seat from the weariness that flowed over him, Dave Kelsey pushed his sight through the gathering dusk. Then he lifted a long arm and pointed off to the south and west.

'That way,' he said shortly. 'Another ninety miles or so and then we reach Big Stone Gap.'

'Is that a town?' asked the Mexican.

'Right near the borders with Kentucky and Tennessee,' Dave said. 'But first we've got to cross the mountains.'

'That will not be easy,' Don Morengo looked up at the sky to the west. 'There is a storm brewing. We must find shelter for the night.'

Dave eyed the approaching storm clouds where darkness and distance crept in from the horizon. 'I know this country. We'll find nothin' if we go on any further. Ground's too open. We'd better move back into the trees. Used to be some old log cabins there. Miners came here to pan for silver and gold and there were others who wanted to stay away from the haunts of men for reasons of their own.' As he spoke he pulled his mount's head around and eased it off the trail, back into the trees.

'Outlaws?' queried Marengo in surprise.

Dave grinned. 'I guess you could call 'em that. They'd made one mistake in their pasts and for that there could be no goin' back for them. They either had to keep on runnin', stayin' one jump ahead of the law and the bounty hunters, or pull off the trails and hide out in these hills.'

They did not press their mounts but, with the darkness and the impending storm coming in fast from the west, the horses made good progress across a stretch of open ground, through a dense thicket and then up the steep slope of a hill where tress and rocky outcrops made the narrow track wind like a snake-trail. This was a narrow neck of hilly country that thrust its way south from the foothills of the Appalachians. Half an hour later they reached a narrow creek, forded it, moved up into the sloping grey rain which beat into their faces, and came upon the wide clearing abruptly on a shelf of level ground.

Dave reined up his mount as he saw the low-roofed hut on the far edge of the clearing. Cautiously he scanned the host of creeping shadows in the broken land of the shelf. There were tricky overtones here in the deepening dusk which endowed rocks and boulders, stunted trees and bushes, with human forms. That was the trouble with this country. During the day there was little to worry a man; but at night it seemed to come alive and turn on them.

Straining to listen, using all of the skills he had learned the hard way during the war, he tried to sift fact from fancy. There was no smoke issuing from the chimney of the cabin, nor even the smell of smoke hanging in the air.

'Abandoned,' he said finally. They crossed a patch of broomweed, the wind covering all sounds, stepped down in front of the hut. Tethering the animals, Dave followed Marengo inside. The smell of a long-deserted place came to meet them, the acrid stench of the dust lifted by their feet and other stale smells which clung to the place. Something scurried with tiny scratching sounds over the hummocky earthen floor, paused for a moment to glare at them out of red, malevolent eyes, then vanished into the gloom in one corner.

'We shall have company during the night,' said Don Marengo, 'but anything would be better than having to stay outside in that storm.'

Thunder rolled over the hills in the distance and a brilliant flash of lighting lit up the interior of the cabin as bright as day. Dave winched and blinked involuntarily.

'Better see about getting something to eat,' he muttered. 'Reckon I could find some wood and get the stove going. Don't fancy sleeping cold and hungry.'

During the night the westerly wind picked up in violence on its long sweep down from the summits of the Appalachians and became a thunder-laden gale, driving the wind against the sides of the cabin, so that water penetrated every crack and split in the logs of which the place was constructed. The shrill gusts bent low every tree and bush, rattling the boards of the cabin so that, in his dreams, as he lay on the low bunk near the stove in the centre of the solitary room, Dave imagined he was in the middle of a Yankee charge in the thicket-strewn wilderness. Haunting his dreams, the thunder became the gigantic roll of cannon fire and he tossed uneasily on the hard bunk, sleeping only fitfully, waking at times during the early hours of the morning, to the moaning wail of the wind and the slashing hammer of the rain at the windows.

Finally he fell into a dreamless sleep and some time during the night the storm must have passed over and the wind abated, for when he woke again it was grey dawn outside and there was a deep stillness over everything. Marengo was still sleeping and, for a long moment, Dave lay with his hands clasped behind his neck, staring up at the low, smoky ceiling. Another day, two at the most, should see him home again. Not that it would be much of a homecoming. He wondered how many things would have changed during the four years he had been away. There had been times, according to some of the rumours which had reached them in camp, that the Union forces had, at times, succeeded in penetrating even as far south as the Tennessee border. He had tried to find out what truth there was in these reports, but without success. There was, at least, one consolation. Perhaps the Yankee carpet-baggers had not got as far south as that yet. It should be possible to salvage something out of the war.

At high noon, two days later, Big Stone Gap lay brooding at the bottom of the draw and, from where he sat, tall in the saddle, Dave saw that there was not too great a change in it since he had ridden out that hot, sultry afternoon, so long ago. There was the long, straggly main street with maybe ten or a dozen intersections, and the square with the large cottonwood in the middle of it, with the low, wooden seat around the base of the trunk, just as he remembered it. A few more houses and stores built around the edge of town, perhaps, and the railroad had finally managed to get through to the northern outskirts. There were, too, fewer gaps between the buildings than he recalled, fewer vacant lots, and the side streets ran further, north and south.

Beyond the town, to the west, the road ran on, straight as a die until it vanished over the summit of the low hill.

Don Marengo said, thoughtfully: 'It looks a nice town, *amigo*. I can understand you wanting to get back.'

'I like it,' Dave nodded. 'The ranch is three miles out of town, over the hill yonder.'

They went down the slope, rode over the plank bridge that spanned the creek, their horses clumping across, and then they were in the main street. There were almost a dozen new saloons now and the bank building had been enlarged to almost twice the size he remembered; a sure sign that the town had, and was still, growing.

At this hour, with the heat head lifting to its noontime pile-up intensity, there were not too many people abroad on the streets. Here, at the bottom of the draw, with the looming hills acting as a natural heat trap, it was even more oppressive and stifling than it had been up there on the brow of the hill. Later in the afternoon, unless memory was playing tricks with him, Dave seemed to recall that a cooling breeze blew down from the west, blowing away the superheated air of high noon, bringing coolness to the evenings.

Keeping a tight grip on the reins, Dave let his glance flick from one side of the street to the other, as they walked their horses towards the centre of town. Four men were seated in high-backed chairs on the boardwalk outside the Twin Ford saloon, hats tilted forward over their faces; yet in spite of this, Dave was certain he and Don Marengo were being closely scrutinised as they rode by.

Just across from the bank a new store had been erected since the time Dave had known the town. There was a wide glass window, shining brilliantly in the sunlight, and in tall, gilt letters which glittered even more brightly than the window itself, the words, 'South Virginia Land Company', and beneath them, in somewhat smaller letter, the name, 'Clem Tollison, Jnr.'

'That's odd,' he said softly, half to himself. 'I never had any of that family figured for land agents.'

'You know them?' inquired Marengo.

'They own the big spread to the north of ours.' Dave pursed his lips. Judging by the expensive look of the building compared with most of the others in its neighbourhood, acting as a land agent was a lucrative business here in Big Stone Gap. Evidently a lot of things had been happening while he had been away. Bitterly, the thought crossed his mind that while he and others had been enduring the rigours of war, there had been men who had remained in comfort back home, lining their pockets at the expense of those who had fought to retain this way of life.

He let his glance wander along the street which stretched towards the square. A tall man, square-shouldered, dressed in black garb, stood in the entrance of the bank, watching them closely as they rode down the street. Dave had seen him a few moments earlier, making his way across the dusty street to the bank, had seen him pause before going inside. Then he had stopped in the act to watch them.

As they drew level with him, Dave returned the man's appraising stare, tried to place the other, but the man was a stranger to him. Smiling a little, cynically, the other took out a cigar, placed it between his lips but did not light it, merely using it as an excuse to watch. Ten yards further on Dave turned in the saddle, but by that time the man had gone and the bank door was swinging shut behind him.

Stepping down in front of the saloon at the edge of the square, they were on the point of going inside when the sound of quick footsteps echoing on the slatted wooden boardwalk caused Dave to jerk up his head in sudden surprise.

'Dave, Dave Kelsey!'

Startled and jolted for a moment, Dave stared at the other without recognition, then realised who the man was. The years had not dealt lightly with him and he seemed to have aged fifteen years, rather than four.

'Flint Enwell.' He grasped the other's hand, shook it, then released it. 'But what has happened to you? You look like a man with all of the world's worries on your shoulders.'

For a long moment Enwell did not answer. Then his words came in a low, dispirited tone. 'Could be you're right at that, Dave. Things have changed a lot since you rode out to the war, but I guess you've found that out for yourself by now.'

'I've found nothing,' Dave retorted. 'I've just ridden in,

on my way out to the ranch after a drink in the saloon. Maybe you'd care to join us.'

There was a sudden flicker of something at the back of the older man's eyes that was not unnoticed by Dave. Outwardly, there seemed to be no change, but Enwell's face had altered, subtly but definitely.

'You've not been out to the ranch yet,' muttered the other. 'Then you haven't seen—' The words ran themselves off into thin nothingness.

'Seen what?' Dave asked. There was a sharp stab of something akin to fear in his mind as he stared at the other, trying to read the expression on his face.

'Reckon I will have that drink with you after all,' Enwell said. He turned sharply, pushed open the saloon door and went inside without pausing to see whether the others were following him. Dave threw a swift glance at Don Marengo, then went inside.

Enwell said nothing until the three of them were seated at one of the tables. Then he said in a thin voice: 'A lot of things have changed here while you've been away, Dave. Bad things.' The other had something to tell him, but the telling of it was clearly a hard thing to accomplish: it lifted the pitch of his voice and laid a tightness around his mouth. 'The Tollisons were at the back of it all. They tried to buy up the ranch from your Pa. Made him an offer and, when he refused to sell out to 'em, they got their men together and rode in one night.'

The other broke off, gulped down his beer, stared down at it for several moments, making no attempt to continue.

Finally Dave said sharply: 'Go on, man. What happened?'

'They put a torch to the place, burned everythin' to the ground. They took your Pa out and shot him down in the courtyard. The others they shot as they tried to get out of the blaze.'

Dave sat wholly still as the other told him; his lips stretched into a thin and somewhat unbelieving line, very tight. Slowly his eyes changed, opening fully on the other as the truth penetrated, staring straight at him with an expression that Enwell could not understand, never afterwards understood. At that moment it was as if he hated everyone in the world. Then he sucked in a long gust of wind, let it out softly in slow pinches through his nostrils.

'I'm sorry I had to be the one to break this news to you,' said Enwell quietly. 'I only wish it could have been otherwise. But when you said you'd just rode in, I figured it would be better you should hear it from me than from any of the others in town, and before you saw the ranch for yourself.'

'And Tollison? What happened to him? Is he still alive?'

Enwell lifted his head, nodded briefly. 'Alive and kickin'. Either the law won't touch him, or it daren't.'

'You mean he wasn't arrested and tried for murder?' It was Marengo who spoke, his tone shocked.

'That's it. Remember all this occurred two years ago. The war was still being fought. So many things were happening around here. The Union forces were less than two miles away and the Confederates were fallin' back fast. Old Man Tollison sure picked the best time to make his play. Claimed the Kelseys were rebels and traitors, that their land was forfeit to the Union. Weren't much anybody could do to stop 'em.'

Dave thought of it slowly. The initial shock was still there, numbing his mind, but there was a saving anger blazing up inside him, making it possible to think more clearly now, his mind reaching around it for the truth. It came to him slowly, hardening his face and mouth, darkening the look on his craggy features. On top of the table his fingers curled into clawed talons, knuckles standing out whitely under the skin from the pressure he was exerting. He wanted to get to his feet, hurl his chair on to the floor and ride out to the Tollison place, kill them all.

'What are you going to do now, *amigo*?' asked Marengo in a soft tone.

Before Dave could answer, Enwell said quickly: 'Get out of town, Dave. If you stay here, they'll come for you. You can't take on the Tollisons and hope to come out on top. Right now, they figure you're dead. It's been some time since the war ended, and when you didn't come back, they spread it around that you'd either been killed or taken prisoner. Even if you were still alive, they said you were a traitor, that you'd never dare show your face here again.'

'But I am here. I did come back.' Dave spoke in a deceptively mild tone; as if this was something which barely interested him, scarcely touched him. 'If there's no law here that will make them pay for what they did, then I must do it myself.'

Enwell shook his head sadly. 'That's what I figured you'd say. In a way, I'm sorry for you. Not because of what has happened, but because of what is goin' to happen if you try to go through with this. The war has left you empty. How do you reckon this chore will leave you, even if you do manage to live through it?'

Dave glanced at him. 'That's strange talk from you, Enwell,' he said. 'You used to be my father's best friend. Now you're tryin' to tell me to ride out and do nothin' to avenge his murder.'

'I'm not tryin' to tell you anythin', Dave. This is a bad homecomin' for you. I know that. You'll hunt and you'll kill if you can, and you won't rest until you've balanced the book for your family.' He paused, drained the last of the beer from the glass, set it down in front of him. 'I'm not arguin' against you, Dave. I'm only tryin' to make you see what you're up against. You'll get no help from the law in Big Stone Gap. Tollison and Ben Chapman, the sheriff, are thicker'n thieves. You'll be branded a traitor and an outlaw as soon as they find out you're still alive. Everybody will be against you.'

'There must be someone who knew my father, who'll stand up against the Tollisons.'

'Nary a one, son,' said Enwell positively. 'Take my word for it. Nobody is goin' to risk all they have just to help you.

They've all forgotten it by now, and they don't want it brought up again.'

'How can a town possibly forget anythin' like this?'

'They can forget.' Enwell pushed back his chair, got to his feet. 'The Tollisons ride herd here. A man tries to go against 'em and he winds up in some gully with a slug in him, or danglin' on the end of a riata. A few tried it when they started takin' over most of the rangeland but they didn't last long.'

'So everybody is scared of the Tollisons.'

'That's right.' Enwell took a step away from the table, cast a furtive glance in the direction of the doors. Now his manner changed. 'Take my advice and get out of Big Stone Gap – right now.'

Turning swiftly on his heel, as though he was aware that he had already said far too much, he hurried across the room, thrust open the batwing doors and went outside. Scarcely had he gone than the doors opened again, swinging slowly aside, letting in the hot sunlight. Three men stood framed in the doorway, two of them holding the batwing doors aside in their hands. The man in the middle, framed by the two rannies, was tall, stockily-built, handsome in a flashy sort of way, as were the clothes he wore. There was a pearl-handled Colt in the holster at his side, a dude's gun, but from the look of the man himself, he seemed the type who knew how to use it.

Dave felt a sudden quickening of his pulses as he recognised the man. Four years had passed but there was no mistaking Jeb Tollison. For a moment the three men paused there, then stepped inside, letting the doors swing shut behind them. They moved slowly over to the bar and, although none of them glanced in Dave's direction, he knew that all three of them were aware of his presence there, knew who he was.

Forcing down the savage anger which rode him, Dave poured himself a shot of whisky, drank it down in a single gulp.

From ten feet along the bar, Tollison said suddenly, loudly: 'Reckon Clinton was right. Didn't believe him at first when he said that yellow skunk Kelsey was not only still alive, but he'd had the gall to ride back into town. Guess some folk will never learn to keep their noses out of trouble.'

Dave caught Marengo's warning glance, bit down the sharp retort that rose to his lips. At the bar, Tollison turned slowly, leisurely, a sneering grin on his face.

'You hear what I said, Kelsey?'

Dave smiled thinly, looked up, completely on balance now, his seething fury held down by his iron will. He knew that the other was deliberately taunting him, waiting for him to make a rash move, possibly so that his two hirelings might shoot him down and claim it was done in self-defence.

'Sure, I heard you. What of it?'

Tollison moved away from the bar, stood in the middle of the room, grinning. 'I allow that it doesn't look right to have a man like you back here in Big Stone Gap, Kelsey. I think somebody should do somethin' about it.'

Dave smiled thinly. 'Meanin' you, Tollison?'

'Could be.' The other's eyes widened a little and he braced his legs, letting his right hand play around his belt buckle. 'Trouble is, I reckon shootin' is too good for the likes of you. We've got ways of taking care of traitors.'

Tollison was still speaking when Dave moved, so swiftly that he was out of his chair and standing beside the table before anyone realised it. His right hand hovered a few inches above the gun butt in his belt.

'If you feel lucky and want to go for your gun, Tollison, reckon you'd better make your play. You figurin' on those two rannies backin' you?'

'They won't make any trouble, Dave.' Turning his head slightly, Dave saw Don Marengo, still seated negligently at the table, but now he had a gun in his hand and it was pointed at the two rannies that stood at the bar. Dave

nodded. 'Well, Tollison? What's the matter? Don't you feel
quite as brave any more now that it's an even fight? Or
maybe you'd prefer it hand to hand?'

Tollison's tongue flicked out, licked the corner of his
mouth. There was a faint beading of sweat on his forehead
and a little trickling down his cheek. For a moment his
gaze slid past Steve, rested on the Mexican at the table,
fixed the other with a stare that said plainly he would
remember this man for the rest of his life, would pay him
back for this whenever the opportunity presented itself.

'All right,' he grunted finally. 'Like I said, shootin' is
too goddamn good for the likes of you. I reckon I'd like it
a lot better if I was to batter you into the dirt with my own
fists.'

As he spoke, he unbuckled the heavy gunbelt, its
leather length snaking through his fingers as he tossed it
against the bar. Dave did likewise, dropping the belt at his
feet, stepping forward, as the other advanced. The sneering expression was still on Tollison's handsome features as
he moved it. He was ready for the fight, hungering for it,
confident he could whip the man who faced him and he
had himself braced for it, every muscle in him poised for
action; still, he was a trifle slow as Dave made his first move
and his fist cracked into Tollison's belly before the other
had his arms lifted. It drove all of the wind out of him; his
hands dropped swiftly in an instinctive act to protect
himself, fingers spread fanwise over his stomach. His face
had turned a yeasty grey and his eyes bulged for a moment
as he backed away in a half crouch. The blow had its effect
too on Dave. It was as if some explosion had taken place
inside him, tearing him apart. The knowledge, deep-
rooted and bitter, that this was one of the men who had
helped to kill his family and burn his home was so strong
that it almost sickened him physically. Then, out of that
inner chaos that threatened to override every other
emotion came rage; a burning, cleansing thing that wiped
his mind clear of all else. Rage! Cold and utterly malig-

nant, flaming with an intensity that shook him like a leaf in a storm. Savage, bleak and destroying. . . .

Backing up against the bar, Tollison stood there for a moment, teetering on his feet, his mouth wide open as he gasped air down into his tortured, heaving lungs. He stood there in apparent agony, seemingly unable to defend himself. Subsequent action on Dave's part was neither planned nor reasoned. Grinning fiercely, he lunged forward, swung another hard blow at the other's face, but his impetuousness almost proved to be his own undoing. Tollison had not been quite as badly hurt as he had made out. Even as Dave swung forward, the other's left arm reached out and grabbed a whiskey bottle off the top of the bar, swung it sideways at Dave's head.

He ducked instinctively, moving away, but even so the end of the bottle caught him a glancing blow on the side of the head and he was unable to ride the stunning force of it completely. Stars blazed in front of his clouded vision and he felt himself falling back head ringing. Acting impulsively, without conscious thought, he smashed his right arm against the other's upraised arm. More by luck than judgment, his clenched first caught the other's wrist, jarring it back against the edge of the bar. Tollison uttered a shrill yelp of agony, dropped the bottle, letting it smash on the floor at his feet.

Even though he had lost his main weapon, at that moment Tollison was in better shape than Dave. His fingers were spread like taloned claws and his puffed lower lip hung open beneath his bloodied nose and mouth. Shuffling forward, no longer quite as sure of himself but wary and still dangerous, he sent in two hard, jabbing rights to Dave's chest, driving him back. His lips were drawn back now over his teeth like those of an animal, his breathing hard. Lowering his head, he came in with a rush, arms wide, clutching Dave around the middle as he bore him backward. The edge of a table rammed with an agonising force into Dave's back, his legs went from under him, and a moment later the flimsy table smashed under their combined weight. He went down with the bigger man on top of him. An unintelligible growl came from the depths of Tollinson's throat as it came to him in that moment that he had got his man just where he wanted him. Shifting his arms, he straddled Dave's chest, moved his fingers up to the other's throat and began to press in savagely with his thumbs.

Dave was starved for air, the effort to drag it down into his lungs was a rasping, laboured attempt to keep himself alive. Blackness hovered in front of his vision and his eyeballs bulged out of their sockets as the big man increased the pressure. He knew that he had to break this hold soon or perish. Already he could feel his last remnants of strength slipping away from him.

Instinctively, he relaxed abruptly. Feeling him go limp, Tollison grinned fiercely and for a second loosened his hold as he bent forward. It was the only chance that Dave would get and he knew it. Tensing the muscles of his arms and legs, he thrust out his limbs in a sudden paroxysm of motion which took Tollison completely unawares. Shaken and jolted, they both came to their feet at the same time and faced each other, Dave already convulsed by his deep-seated anger and Tollison warming up to the same emotion. As he eyed his adversary warily, Dave had his first clear flash of what he was up against. He had started something here and it was going to take a great deal to finish it. Tollison, for all his fancy appearance, was a strong man and, as yet, his endurance had hardly been touched. His face was blotched with crimson from his split lips and there was a deep graze down the side of his cheek but, apart from these minor injuries, he was still tremendously strong; and the beating his features had taken had made him all the more determined to punish the man responsible.

Dave did not give the other the chance to pick his own time but went in fast, dodging beneath a chopping blow, taking a second one on his left shoulder, and then straightening up to smash his clenched fist in the other's throat. It was a murderous blow that shook the big man, dazed him, sent him rocking back on his heels, mouth opening and closing like a fish out of water as he struggled to get air down into his lungs.

Dave did not wait for the other to recover from the effect of the blow. He drove forward, hammering the other back against the bar. His fist smacked into the other's belly, driving deep into the flesh, doubling Tollison up as he strove to move away, to slide along the bar.

Tollison took two more savage blows to the face before he got one in himself, a hammer-fisted jab that half-spun Dave around and gave Tollison a short breathing space in which to collect his scattered wits. Dave hammered at him again, but the blows only halted the other's advance by a single stride, and he was forced to give ground fast, trying to get his own whirling mind and vision into focus again, knowing that this was going to be a fight to the finish, with no quarter asked and none given on either side.

He had taken two steps back towards the middle of the room when he suddenly realised that the other had not taken advantage of this, was not moving in close. Through his blurred vision, he saw the vicious grin on Tollison's face, saw his right hand move towards his coat. It was then he knew that the other had only dropped his gunbelt because he carried another gun in a shoulder holster. A small Derringer, perhaps, a woman's gun, but one which at that range would be lethal.

Chance alone saved Dave Kelsey at that point. The barrel of the gun caught in the lining of the other man's coat. Savagely he tugged at it. Even as Dave lunged forward, there was the ripping of cloth as the weapon came free. The sunlight glinting on blue metal, the barrel of the Derringer was already swinging up towards his chest when he drove a shoulder into the man, hurling his off balance, cornering him against the bar. Grabbing at Tollison's wrist, he twisted sharply, felt the bone crack under the skin. The Derringer bellowed once and the flame of it was a licking lance of light and heat close to Dave's face. He felt the wind of the bullet near his cheek. A window of the saloon tinkled into a hundred fragments that fell on to the floor with a thin, brittle sound at his back.

Savagely Dave kneed the other and there was a bleating agony in Tollison's cry of pain as he doubled forward. With his free right fist Dave clubbed him brutally behind the ear, driving him fully down. Half-conscious, Tollison thrust his arms out in front of him in an effort to break his fall, floundering on his hands and knees like some stricken animal, head rocking forward on his neck. He tried feebly to grab at Dave's legs as he knelt there, struggling to upset him and throw him back. Straightening his hand, Dave hit him with all the force he could muster on the back of the neck. A weaker neck would have snapped under the shuddering impact of that driving blow. As it was, Tollison uttered a faint murmur of sound, then pitched forward on to his face. He was completely unconscious before his face hit the dirt of the floor.

That finished it. The fight had been savage, hard and brutal. Now Tollison lay hunched and inert on the floor, arms and legs doubled up under him. Dave stepped back, panting a little from the exertion. A trickle of blood oozed down from his cut lip and he rubbed at it angrily. The fury which had prompted this fight still burned in him, but he felt a little better than before. The desire to kill Tollison in cold blood was no longer there; far better to let him live, to go through the next few weeks, or months, knowing that inexorably his death would come very soon, but not knowing when or where.

Even when it is a silent thing, a grim battle between two men breeds its own atmosphere of violence, giving it off like the unmistakable reck of gunsmoke, touching the nerves of men in the vicinity, forcing them to watch, eagerly and avidly.

Brushing back the hair which had fallen in front of his eye, Dave looked about him. The two rannies were still standing against the bar. They did not appear to have moved a single muscle during the whole course of the fight. Stooping to pick up his gunbelt, he fastened it on, then said curtly: 'All right, you two. Pick him up and get him out of here. And tell your boss that Dave Kelsey is back in town. He'll understand.'

Without a word, the two gunmen moved forward, picked up the unconscious Jeb Tollison and carried him out of the saloon. Not until they had gone did Dave finally relax. The saltiness of blood was in his mouth and on his lips. He did not recall the blow which had put it there. Spitting it out, he rubbed his mouth with the back of his hand.

'That was a good fight while it lasted, *amigo*,' said Don Marengo. He poured a glass of whisky, set it in front of the other as he sat down.

'One of those things,' he said, harshly brief. 'But it's only the beginning.'

Don Marengo's face was grimly thoughtful. Finally he said, 'I must sympathise with you, Dave, for what had happened. This is not the homecoming you thought. These men will not stop until they have destroyed you utterly. You know that of course.'

Dave laughed a dry, humourless sound. Tossing the drink down in a single gulp, he slammed the empty glass on to the table. Anger thinned his lips momentarily. Glancing up, he noticed the bartender watching him curiously. Abruptly he got to his feet, walked over to the other, resting his elbows on the bar.

'Reckon you know what's been goin on around Big Stone Gap these past few years,' he said ominously. 'Want to tell me about it?'

The other stood behind the counter, drearily polishing glasses. He stood a moment, staring at Dave, inwardly making a test of his courage. It was obvious from the look

in his eyes that he was afraid of the Tollisons; and yet he
had seen one of them battered into unconsciousness by
this man who stood before him. Presently he dropped his
eyes.

'You know who I am?' Dave said tightly.

'Sure. You're Dave Kelsey. They said you'd been killed
in the war.'

'That's what they'd like to think, what they'd like you to
believe. Now you know different, are you goin' to tell me
what happened?'

The other gave him a sour, half-worried look. 'You
know the Tollisons,' he said eventually. 'Old Clem Tollison
has been wantin' to get his hands on all of the land around
town ever since he came here twenty or more years ago.
Only your Pa was big enough and strong enough to stop
him. After you'd gone, he took to studying some of the
land grants of the smaller folk in the territory, hired a
lawyer from somewhere up north, looked for legal flaws in
the old deeds. Seems he found some, got 'em declared
void in the court here and filed his own claims to the land.
Weren't nothin' the folk could do about it. Everythin'
seemed legal and, with the Union forces headin' this way,
nobody was in any condition to fight except your father.'

'So Tollison had to get him out of the way before he
could go ahead.'

'Somethin' like that, I guess. The owners of some of the
spreads tried to fight Tollison by takin' their cases to the
other courts. Reckon they may have got the decisions here
reversed, but it took time and, by then, Tollison and his
sons had built up quite an army of hired guns. The time
the owners took tryin' to do things accordin' to the law
had all been wasted. Tollison moved in and took 'em over
by force. A few killings on the range, a few hangings here
in town, one or two so-called accidents, and all the heart
went out of anybody who tried to fight. Then when
Tollison threw in his lot with the Union, it really was the
end. He had the army to back him up. Nobody dared go

against 'em, with the Confederates in full flight to the west.'

'What happened that night they killed my family?' Dave tried to keep his tone even and casual.

'Don't know the full story of that. Only what I heard in here. They'd made their plans well.' He spoke through quick, short lifts of his breath eyes continually flicking in the direction of the batwing doors as if expecting the Tollisons to come marching through in a bunch. 'Hit your place just after midnight, killed a couple of guards, then moved in on the ranch. Your Pa put up a fight, but he was surprised and outnumbered. After they'd dragged him out into the courtyard and shot him, they put a torch to the building, waited until—' He broke off uncomfortably as he saw the look in Dave's eyes, licked his lips as though his mouth were suddenly dry.

'Go on,' said Dave roughly. 'I want to know all of it.'

'They waited until your mother and the others ran out of the building and then gunned them down in cold blood.' As he finished, the bartender closed his teeth with an audible snap, lips clamped tightly together.

Dave drew in his breath; let it softly out. Don Marengo got to his feet and came over. He said softly: 'If you intend to remain here, you will need help to fight these men.'

Dave smiled bitterly. 'You heard what Enwell said, no one will side with me against the Tollisons.'

'You forget that you did me a great service in Clayton,' replied the other. 'I can bring many *vaqueros* from the south who will fight.

3

The Big Men

The stars of early evening were just beginning to show against the clear dusk sky when the three men rode down out of the low hills, across the flat basin beside the river and on through the grove of tall trees up to the Tollison ranch. Jeb Tollison sat forward in the saddle, his face set in hard, bitter lines. Through the sodden thickness of his thoughts he was recalling that the bartender and at least two other men in the saloon had seen him get a thrashing at Kelsey's hands. The knowledge rankled deep within him. It was still difficult for him to remain upright in the saddle. His body was a mass of aches and bruises and there was dried blood congealed on the side of his face where an open cut still bled whenever he tried to wash the crust of blood away.

From time to time he turned his head slowly and stared at the two men who rode with him, trying to judge their thoughts from the looks on their faces, wondering if they too were laughing at him inwardly. It was the first time in his life that anybody had bested Jeb Tollison in a square fight. Very soon the news was going to get around town and he writhed with an inner torment.

A vain and utterly ruthless man, the events of the past day were like acid burning at his mind. He had been so

sure that he could take Kelsey that he had gone into the
rough and tumble with his eyes open, confident and arrogant.

Riding over a plank bridge across the river, they turned
into the quiet courtyard. With a slow care, he stepped
down from the saddle, wincing as every movement sent
pain searing through his limbs. Leaving his mount to the
men, he made his cautious way towards the house. For a
moment he paused at the top of the steps, holding tightly
on to the porch rail, drawing long, slow gusts of air into his
lungs as his head swam. Then he went up on to the porch,
feeling steadier now.

Thrusting open the door, he stumbled inside, made his
way slowly to the parlour. Clem Tollison, silver-haired, his
face still handsome in spite of his fifty-eight years, glanced
up from the table as he came in, then got swiftly to his feet.

'Creede! Mer!' The older man hurried over, helped
him to a chair. 'Who did this, Jeb?'

'Dave Kelsey. I met up with him in the saloon in town.
He had some Mexican hombre with him. While the Mex
held a gun on me, he beat me up. The boys could do
nothin' to help.'

Clem Tollison's eyes grew very still and in their grey
depths a great wrath moved slowly. 'Kelsey!' His tone was
thin. 'You're sure it was Kelsey?'

Jeb nodded. 'Of course I'm sure,' he muttered testily.
'He even bragged about it, said he was here for one reason
– to finish us for what we did to his family.'

Clem straightened up as the outer door opened.
Creede Tollison was similar in height and build to Jeb,
whereas his brother Merl was shorter, thinner, his face
angular, dark eyes empty and devoid of expression, glittering in the dimness like those of a snake about to strike.
Of all the Tollisons, he alone preferred to discard the
dressy clothes the others wore for a dark shirt and chaps
like an ordinary cowboy, a broad leather gunbelt slung low
around his waist, twin Colts thrust in to the holsters.

'Seems that Dave Kelsey wasn't killed in the war,' growled Tollison harshly. 'He just rode into town with some Mexican. Jeb here had a run-in with him in the saloon.'

Creede said nothing, merely stared down at the blood-smeared face of his brother. Merl grinned viciously. He said harshly: 'Somehow I always figured he might show up some time. I've been waitin' for this. You want me to take a few of the boys and ride into town tonight?'

'No!' The older man's tone was sharp. He lifted his head and made a strange upward jerk with it. 'We've got to go about this the right way. The war's finished. The Union forces are here but they won't back us this time in an act of murder. We've come a long way in the past few years and I don't intend to throw away everything we gained by any rash act.'

Crede broke in: 'He could become dangerous if we leave him alive too long.'

His father shook his head slowly. 'There's nobody in the territory will lift a finger to help him. He's a man riding alone. We'll take him in our own good time. Remember that. I'm tellin' you to leave him until I'm good and ready to finish him. His father was a stone around my neck for too long for me to forget everythin' I owe the Kelseys. This man is the last of the line. When he's dead, it will be the end of them for good and all. But I want him to suffer a little before he dies. I want him to have to wonder, every minute of every day and night, just when we make our move against him. All I'm asking of you is to keep an eye on his movements and ride a wide circle around him.'

'And that Mex who's riding with him?' muttered Jeb thickly. He shook his head to clear it.

The other pondered that for a moment, then said: 'Watch him, too. If he sticks with Kelsey, then I figure it's only right that he should suffer the same fate. Tomorrow morning I'm riding into town to have a word with Ben Chapman. It won't be difficult to have Kelsey branded as an outlaw as well as a traitor.'

Getting to his feet, Jeb stood swaying for a moment, gripping the edge of the nearby table tightly to keep himself upright. 'Just one thing, Father,' he said hoarsely.

The other looked at him broodingly, already engrossed in his own thoughts. 'Well?'

'When you do decide to kill him, I want the job. I reckon you owe it to me after what he did today in the saloon.'

The other paused for a moment, then nodded. 'If you reckon you can take him, then he'll be yours,' he said. For a moment there was a cynical grin on his lined features. 'Now you'd better get your face cleaned up.'

Dave Kelsey made his way slowly along the main street of Big Stone Gap shortly before ten o'clock the next morning. An hour earlier Don Ricardo Marengo had ridden out, heading south, after promising to collect some of his *vaqueros* and bring them north with him. Dave had accepted the offer gratefully. He fully appreciated the difficulties and dangers which faced him now, in a town and surrounding territory which were so ominously hostile to him. He had ridden here believing that there was nothing further for him to do but start his life anew virtually where he had left off to ride to the war. Now he was completely alone in the world, among men whose only desire was to kill him. For a moment his thoughts ran fast and uncertain in his mind and the memory of how his whole family had been wiped out was a growing, gnawing, bitter fury which refused to be stilled. The fact that the law here had actually condoned these cold-blooded murders and left the killers free to go their way unhindered, even to enjoy their ill-gotten gains, rankled even more.

It was like a knife twisting deep inside him, and he knew the pain of it would never ease, the dragging spurs of anger would never leave him, until every last Tollison was dead and the debt had been repaid in blood.

He crossed the street, walking slowly with the stiffness of the previous day's fight still in his bones, the bruises on his flesh. He was hungry and looked about him for the nearest place where he might get something to eat and drink. Somewhere to sit down, stretch his legs, and try to get his thoughts and ideas into some kind of order. Already, as far as he knew, there might be a plan in the making against him and he would have to be prepared to meet it.

Clancy's saloon was open but, as he drew level with the door, he heard the sound of voices and raucous laughter inside, even at that early hour of the day. Smoke and noise, and the open, curious stares of the townsfolk were something he didn't want just then and he walked on. He recalled a little eating place along the narrow side street that led off from the far side of the square. Maybe it was still open after all these years. In the old days, before the war had come to change so many things, it had been run by a strange man, Thomas Herbison; strange perhaps because he was an Englishman who had come over to America some ten years before and opened this small place in Big Stone Gap, starting the restaurant from nothing. He had never really prospered, but in the intense and bitter rivalry between the Kelseys and the Tollisons, he had remained utterly neutral, taking no sides. Somehow, he felt sure that, in spire of his little idiosyncracies. Herbison could be trusted.

He opened the door of the restaurant and almost bumped into Herbison himself coming out.

'Too early for somethin' to eat, Thomas?'

The other stared at him for a long moment and slowly a look of surprised recognition dawned over his square features. 'Dave Kelsey!' He grinned and then sobered, a dark look replacing the expression of welcome. 'I'm sorry about what happened, boy.'

'Thanks. Can I get something to eat?'

'Sure. Stacy is still there. She'll fix you up with something.' He paused on the step, brows drawn together. 'Like to have a talk with you before you ride out, son.'

Dave nodded. 'I'll still be here when you get back.'

The small restaurant was empty as Dave stepped inside. In the street the heat had already begun to make itself felt, with a hot, dust-laden wind blowing in from the southwest, but here it was shady and cool. Glancing around him, he noticed that only one of the tables had been set and there were a few dishes still on it. Probably Herbison had been taking his breakfast there, rather than in the back, figuring it would be a little while before he got any customers.

He paused for a moment in the silence, then walked softly around the edge of the counter towards the door which led into the kitchen at the rear of the building. The faint sound of his spurs was the only thing to disturb the stillness, but just as he laid his hand on the knob of the door, a soft voice from inside the further room said: 'That you, Dad?'

Dave hesitated for a moment, then pushed open the door and went into the kitchen, looking about him. There was the appetising smell of frying bacon and hot roasted coffee in the air, reminding him anew of how hungry he was. Stacy Herbison was standing in front of the iron stove, her back to him. For a moment Dave felt a sudden sense of surprise at seeing her. When he had last known her she had been little more than a girl with pigtails hanging down her back. Now she seemed to be a grown woman, with all the womanly charms. She turned as he stood there, saying nothing, her eyes widening for a moment in alarm.

'Who—?' she began.

'It's me, Stacy. Dave Kelsey.'

'Dave, but—'

'I know.' He moved towards her. 'There's been a lot of

talk about me being killed in the war.' His eyes clouded a little. 'Maybe it would have been better for me if I had.'

Instinctively she came to him, placed a hand on his arm. 'Sit down, Dave. I'll get you something to eat. Then you can talk.'

'Thanks, Stacy.' He watched her appraisingly as she went back to the stove, took down some bacon and placed it in the pan. She was silent for a long time, her head bent forward a little so that the long chestnut hair covered it. Then she said, very softly: 'You've heard what happened?'

'I met Flint Enwell yesterday just after I rode in. He told me.' He tried to keep the anger and bitterness out of his voice, but it was impossible.

She turned away from the stove, set the plate in front of him, brought him bread and coffee, then seated herself in the chair opposite, leaning toward a little over the table, watching him eat, feeling the deep hurt that was in him, knowing with a sort of feminine instinct that right now there was very little she could do or say which would help.

'Tastes good,' he said after a pause.

'I'm glad. Dad often says he's a better cook than I am.'

'Then he's wrong.' He glanced at her, still scarcely able to believe this was the same girl he had known four years before. It just didn't seem credible that she could have grown into such a beautiful woman. He remembered, with a faint flush, that in those days she had been a tomboy, had used a gun and ridden a horse with the best of them. He wondered if she ever thought back to those days, or whether the intervention of the war had brought a curtain down on that past life as it had for so many others Dave knew.

He ate the bacon, wiped up the fat with his bread, then sat back, making himself a cigarette, rolling it between his fingers with an oddly absent motion as if his thoughts were elsewhere.

'Business still slow in town?' He asked, lighting the cigarette and blowing the blue smoke towards the ceiling.

'Some,' she admitted. 'We generally do a lot better in the evenings and on Saturdays. This is the slack time.'

'The town's growin' fast. Seems they've been buildin' a lot out to the north.'

'Now that the war is over, everybody is trying to get things really going again. There are still plenty of hungry mouths to feed and we ship a lot of beef out to the markets north and west of here.'

'The Tollisons still doin' a lot?'

He saw the cloudy look on her face, waited for her to speak. She was silent for several moments, lips pressed together, long and heavy. 'They're big men now, Dave. Bigger and more powerful than you remember them. Oh, they had plenty of cattle and land before the war, but Old Man Tollison saw the way things were going more clearly and long before most of the others. He meant to be on the winning side when the war ended and he planned for it. Now he's got so many men workin' on his payroll that nobody dares to go against him. Those who've tried it in the past have either been killed or forced to pull out.' She added the last slowly, intending it as a warning to him.

'And the law here in Big Stone Gap?'

'Ben Chapman is a weak-willed man. Tollison forced him into the post of sheriff. Mabon, the Mayor, had to back his appointment whether he liked it or not.'

Dave remembered Carl Mabon. The other had always struck him as a straight and honest man, a little unsure of himself in the field of politics, but not as crooked as some. Still, when pressures were brought to bear a man either fell into step or went under. No doubt Mabon had had to face this issue and had decided there was only one thing to do unless he wanted to go the same way as most of the others.

Stacy went on: 'Maybe Chapman doesn't agree with what the Tollisons are doing, but he has no other choice.'

'I'll try to remember that when I meet up with him.'

She sipped her coffee and watched him over the rim of

the cup, studying him in the same manner she had earlier, out of extremely grave eyes. 'What are you going to do now, Dave? If you stay here, they'll kill you. You know that?'

'I know they'll try.'

'Don't ever underestimate them. Make one move and they'll brand you as an outlaw and your own worst enemy. These men will never be better, only worse. But you weren't born to be like that. You weren't meant to snap and snarl at the world like an animal.'

'Even an animal will do all it can to avenge its family if they're killed in cold blood.' He studied the thought and he tried to work his mind around it, closing the fingers of his left hand into a tight fist, squeezing hard until the knuckles stood out whitely under the flesh and the sinews on the back of his arm stood out like cords. He felt unsettled by the depth of his feeling, brought back to him by the terrible memories that rankled in his brain.

Draining his coffee, he pushed back his chair and rose to his feet. 'How much do I owe you, Stacy?'

'Nothing, Dave. You know that.' She got up, too, stood beside him, her head higher than his shoulder. 'I know how you feel and I don't blame you. But be careful. These men have too much to lose, too much at stake, for them to think twice about killing you. And you can't hope to fight them alone.'

'I've got friends,' he said bluntly.

She did not understand him, shook her head slowly, hopelessly. 'Not here in town. Not friends who will help you fight the Tollisons.'

'No, I realise that. But I have other friends as they'll discover to their cost,' he said enigmatically. He noticed the look on her face and instinctively put out a hand, holding her arm. She did not move away. 'Don't worry on my account, Stacy. I can take care of myself.'

'I hope so.' She sounded dubious as she followed him from the room, stood in the kitchen doorway watching him walk among the empty tables to the street door, his head down and his shoulders sloped.

With the heat of high noon glaring down on the dusty street, Dave Kelsey sat in the high-backed chair on the boardwalk in front of the hotel, his hat tilted on the back of his head, watching the far end of the street. He had made himself calm now, the icy fury buried deep in his mind, buried but not forgotten. He wiped his face with his bandanna. Just take it easy, he told himself. No point in going off half-cocked against these ruthless men. That was undoubtedly what Tollison would be wanting him to do. Move quickly and fall into a trap. Just calm down. Keep your eyes and ears open and wait for Herbison to put in an appearance.

A couple of riders moved into town from the opposite end of the street, reined up in front of the bank and went inside. Dave gave them a cursory glance and then went back to watching the other stretch of street, the white dust glaring wickedly in his eyes.

It was almost an hour later before Thomas Herbison put in an appearance. Dave did not see where he had come from. One moment the street was empty, the next Herbison was striding purposefully along the middle of it, ignoring the blistering heat that poured down from the inverted furnace of the noon heavens.

Getting to his feet, Dave stepped down into the street. Almost at once, moving out of the shade, the full force of the heat hit him. He had never known it to be as hot here in Virginia.

'You normally go out at this time of day, Thomas?' He asked as the other drew level with him.

Herbison grunted something unintelligible. He fell into step with Dave. 'Hoped you'd stick around until I got a chance to talk to you. Now that you know what's been goin' on around here, I can figure what you mean to do.'

'So?'

'So there are some things you should know before you get that fool head of yours blown off.' He rubbed the back of his hand across his stubbled chin. 'I heard about that ruckus in the saloon with Jeb Tollison. Was that a smart thing to do?'

'What would you have had me do in the circumstances? Let him stand there and talk his big mouth off?'

Herbison shrugged. 'Maybe not. But Old Man Tollison is already spreading it around that your Pa rustled nearly a thousand head of his beef, forcing him to move against him. Some of that is going to stick to you, boy. Won't be too hard for him to have you branded as an outlaw. How far do you think you'll get with both Tollison and his men and the law on your heels?' Sombreness was on the older man and harshness pulled his lined face into grim contours.

'Far enough. Tollison doesn't know it yet, but pretty soon he won't be gettin' things all his own way.'

'I hope you've got something more up your sleeve than an ace. They're a mean bunch, Dave. And whatever it is, in the meantime you'll be a walking target for any of 'em. You staying in town?'

'I'm riding out tonight. In a case like this, I want them to come to me. They won't be expectin' that and it may throw 'em a little.'

Herbison's eyes narrowed a little as he considered this. 'I've seen a dozen men who thought they were big enough to stand up to the Tollisons coming riding into town and try to set themselves up. Ain't one of 'em stayed more'n a few months. Those who ain't buried on Boot Hill yonder pulled up stakes, cut their losses, and moved out. But there was one big difference between them and you.'

'Oh. What might that be?' Dave asked.

'Tollison just wanted rid of 'em because he was determined to get all of their land for himself and grab off all of the range. He didn't care a damn about the men themselves. They were just men who rode in and tried to put their roots down here where he didn't want them. But as for you. He sure enough wants you dead and he won't rest until you're buried so deep everybody will forget you ever existed.' He turned his grave eyes on Dave, his glance now prodding the other as he tried to measure him up. 'You're not green any longer, Dave. And I reckon the war has probably taught you the same kind of dirty experience it did many of the others.' For a moment caution held the other back, then he went on: 'Evil has to be faced with evil, or a man who's stronger than the others. I'm not sure you're big enough.'

Dave Kelsey rode down from the high hills to the west of Big Stone Gap in the shrieking, wind-snarled night, with the bright stars showing at intervals through gaps torn in the racing clouds and a thin yellow slice of a moon swinging on its back to the east. On either side of him the gaunt, rising folds of the hills crowded close to the trail, the entire weight of the mountains tilted against the road, uprearing, black hummocks of shadow that reared up against the angry night.

Pulling up the collar of his coat, he sat hunched forward in the saddle. Half a mile further on he reached a sharply angled bend in the trail, put his mount down a narrow track which twisted sharply to the right, stretching away from him in the moonlight like a tunnel of blackness, opening out into a wider canyon, with only the sound of his horse's hooves striking the hard rock surface with a metallic clatter to keep him company.

Some time during the early hours of the morning the threatened rain came, driving at him from the upper ridges of the hills, stinging his eyes, lashing at his face so that even when he was bowed forward in the saddle it still struck his flesh, numbing it with its incessant hammering. Down below him he could just make out the dull wash of the river where it wound among the rocks and crags, perhaps two hundred feet below the twisting trail. Sucking in a deep breath, he tried to force the black thoughts from his mind. He scarcely noticed the discomfort of his sodden clothing, the damp shirt which clung to his back, the water which cascaded from the brim of his hat with every movement of his head. The further he made his way down towards the wooden bridge that spanned the river, the less was the force of the turbulent wind, but the rain continued to fall steadily, and there was no shelter from it.

As he rode he felt a tingling renewal of his familiarity with the land. Even in the rain-filled darkness he seemed to remember each arroyo, each rising granite stand, each cluster of trees that lifted on wind-swept ridges, each turn in the river, half-hidden in the night. The long cedar stands, the gullies, were old friends.

Shortly before grey dawn he came down from the hills, on to the edge of the spread which had been his home four years earlier. Now there was an air of desertion about it that struck deep within him. Tumbleweed drifted over the wet earth. The fence which had marked the eastern boundary lay smashed and trampled flat, the strands of wire rusted. Saddle-weary, he let the horse pick its own gait, taking in everything in the dim light.

Presently he topped a low rise, came in sight of the ranch-house. Reining up, he sat hunched forward in the saddle and let his gaze wander over the burnt-out ruins which confronted him. Here was where the story had started and ended, he reflected bitterly. The thought, even now, turned its knife point deep in his bowels. Now that he was here, this was to be his burden, and that burden had changed him, almost overnight. It had burned away all of his easy-going nature, something which even the savagery of the war had not been able to do. It made him tough, sad, disbelieving and full of the blazing need for vengeance.

In the wet, grey dawn he walked through the tumbled, splintered ruins. Even now, after all this time, he thought he still detected the smell of smoke hanging in the air

from the blackened timbers. There was scarcely a wall left
standing, great holes showing in the roof. He remembered how his father had freighted all of the wood down
from the junction to the north when the place had been
built. It made everything seem so damned futile now.

He spent the morning hauling the beams away,
salvaging what wood he could. In the barn he came across
two bags of rusted nails and a hammer. An hour later there
was the sound of sawing and hammering in the wide clearing on the slope of the hill. Occasionally the horse looked
up from where it had been ground-reined in the courtyard, then went back to its grazing on the tufts of grass that
grew up here and there through the hard earth. Dave
Kelsey was home once more.

The lantern light in Clancy's gleamed dully on Merl
Tollison's dark hair and brown face, striking points of
light from the cold eyes. He wore no hat and his thin
hair hung limply on his forehead as he stood with his
elbows resting on the bar. He was speaking to the short,
bony man who stood, glass in hand, beside him, small
eyes as piercing as gimlets, the thin lips compressed into
a tight line. He looked – and was – a highly dangerous
man, wearing two guns on the heavy sagging belt that
hung around his middle, each leather slot filled with
cartridges. Although officially one of the Tollison crew,
he had been hired by Merl some months before and
took orders only from him. Old Man Tollison was aware
of the situation, but regarded Charlie Fenton as too
dangerous a customer to be antagonised, and so long as
what he did was for the good of the Tollison cause in
general, he raised no objections.

A seasoned gunman, who had fought with the rene-
gades during the latter part of the war, his services were for
hire to nearly everyone, provided the price was right.
Wherever trouble was to be fermented, Charlie Fenton

was sure to be around, and there were rumours that he had gunned down his own brother since the price had been right and the risk had not been too apparent. At first acquaintance, one might have been excused for walking a wide circle around him. Though one might have entrusted Merl Tollison with his confidence, nobody ever made that mistake with Fenton.

'Word has it he's out at the ranch,' Merl was saying. 'Seems he rode out two, three days ago.'

'He won't find much there.' The thought amused Fenton. 'We made a good job of that place. Nothin' more'n a handful of ruins by now.'

'What's the opinion in town of Kelsey?'

Fenton took time over his reply. After consideration, he said: 'It's thought he's hell-bent for trouble. Reckon he won't stop until he's either paid off all those who wiped out his family, or he's been stopped himself. It's allowed he's dangerous – packs a gun he knows how to use and acts like he's goin' to use it pretty soon. Could be he learned a lot durin' the war. It turned some *hombres* into hard cases.'

'That your final verdict of him?' Merl pressed him.

The other's narrowed eyes gleamed in derision. 'I reckon he's nothin' more than a brash young colt who came ridin' back expectin' something and found everythin' a heap different from what he'd imagined. I figure he reckons he's better than he is.' Fenton's grin thinned down a little. 'I've met his breed before, plenty of times. I wouldn't mind meetin' him on an even break.'

Merl snorted his satisfaction at this remark. 'Good. Now, here's the way I figure it,' he said briskly, filling their glasses from the bottle at his elbow. 'Natural enough he wants vengeance for what happened. Maybe we made a mistake in guessin' he wouldn't come back. Thing is, if he's anywhere near as good as they say he is, he could make us a lot of trouble. I want us to get rid of him before he can start.'

'Your Pa said he was to be left alone until he was good and ready,' put in Fenton. There was no emotion in his voice. He spoke as if the older man's decision had no interest for him.

'Don't worry. I'll see to it that he knows nothin' about it until it's too late. Once Kelsey is dead, ain't nothing can stand in our way.'

Fenton shrugged. He tossed off the last of his drink. 'When do you figure on doin' it?' he asked incisively.

'The sooner, the better,' declared the other. 'I reckon the two of us can handle him, however good he is.'

The gunman leaned forward on the bar. He lowered his tone a little. 'One point you seem to have overlooked, Tollison.'

'What's that?' grunted Merl. He felt a momentary anger at the way the other spoke to him. There were times, he decided, when Fenton seemed to forget that he was merely a hired hand and not an equal. But he was too good a man to argue with, and Tollison let it pass.

'There's talk that when Kelsey arrived in town, there was a Mex ridin' with him.'

'I heard that,' Merl said irritably. 'But he rode out the next day. Where's the trouble there?'

Fenton looked surprised. 'Don't you see it? Suppose this Mex was a friend of his? Suppose Kelsey knows that there ain't anybody in town who'll lift a finger to help him. Might be the Mex has friends who'll ride with Kelsey.'

Merl dug his tobacco pouch from his pocket, made himself a cigarette. He was forced to admit that this was an eventuality he had not foreseen. He lit the cigarette and puffed deeply on it, removing his eyes from Fenton. 'Then we've got to put an end to Kelsey before this friend of his can get back here with any men.'

Fenton grinned. 'You know, Tollison,' he said speculatively, 'I reckon it's a good thing for you I'm on your payroll. Without me, you'd soon be stretched out on your back in the dirt with a dozen slugs nestlin' in your chest.'

Merl forced down the quick anger. 'You're not cheap, I'll admit,' he muttered finally, 'but I reckon you could say you're a sort of insurance I've got against these unforeseen happenings. You're reliable – and when I need you I want you right there on the spot. That's why I keep you on. Besides, for the moment Kelsey is the danger as I see it. But when he's out of the way, there may be other chores I shall want you to carry out for me. I guess you know what they might be.'

'Sure,' said the other bluntly. 'The plain truth is that your Pa ain't goin' to live for ever. When he dies, somebody has to run the place. No sense in dividin' it if you don't have to, is there?'

Merl blew smoke in front of him, stared at the little gunman through the drifting blue haze. 'Reckon you and me see things in the same light, Fenton.' He nodded. 'You can dust along now. But meet me here tonight at nine. If we ride hard we could reach the old Kelsey place in three hours.'

'If he's still here,' countered the other.

'He'll be there,' said Merl positively. 'He's got a chore to do and, knowin' Kelsey, nothin' is going to stop him doin' it.'

'Reckon he's mad, staying there, knowin' what's bein' stacked up against him,' murmured the other, as he hitched up his sagging gunbelt, turned on his heel and moved out of the saloon.

Mad? thought Merl, watching him go. Somehow, he wasn't sure about that. Even taking into account the desire for revenge that must have been uppermost in Kelsey's mind, a man who would take a risk like this had to be plenty sure of his ability to handle the situation. For the first time, thinking it over, Tollison was beginning to have some doubts as to the invincibility of Charlie Fenton as a fast gun. With an effort, he dismissed the idea angrily from

his mind. Thinking instead of his ambition, of his determination to get the whole of the land for himself once his
father died, his face grew ugly.

4

Clash of Guns

The two men rode through a narrow cut of a dry creek, sheltered from sight by its high, rough banks. Now that they were close to the spot where he expected to find Dave Kelsey, Merl Tollison's mind was filled with a heightened anticipation. He wanted to get it over with, to ride back to the ranch and impart the information to the others. The fact that Jeb had wanted the chore of finishing Kelsey made the thought even more desirable.

'Why'd you figure he's so intent on building this place up again?' muttered Fenton. 'You've got the land about here. Ben Chapman will back your play if you was to run him off.'

'No call to bring the sheriff into this little matter,' said Merl irritably. 'We can deal with it between us. When he's dead, there'll be no problem.'

The creek bed twisted seemingly aimlessly along its steep, gravel like course. When they came to the slope at the far end, Merl called softly: 'Not much further now. Try to keep quiet from here on. I don't want to warn him.'

'Ain't likely he'll be awake and stirrin' at this time of night,' grunted the other. He lapsed into a surly silence. They put their horses to the slope. At the top, mounting into the tall cedars. Here, on this side of the old Kelsey

61

place, Merl saw that the brush had grown a lot thicker than he remembered it from that night when they had ridden in force out of the darkness and destroyed every member of the Kelsey family there, leaving the ranch itself blazing like a funeral pyre, the flames lighting up the dark heavens.

Fifteen minutes later the more open country was cut off by tall rocky upthrusts and, except for a sudden rise of startled quail, the surrounding terrain was still and apparently lifeless. Peering into the dimness, Merl was just able to make out the shadowy patch that marked the position of the ranch. He paused for a moment, holding up his right hand to halt Fenton.

Bending close to the other, he said in a low tone: 'Looks as if he's started rebuilding the place for sure.'

The gunman gave a cursory nod. 'So we fire it again,' he remarked. His tone implied that he did not consider this a problem.

'You stay here while I scout the place,' ordered Tollison, slipping silently from the saddle. He looped the bridle over the out-thrusting branch of one of the nearby stunted trees, padded noiselessly forward, crouching low as he moved.

He paused at times to listen, satisfying himself that there was no sound from within the roughly timbered erection ahead of him. Cautiously he scouted the building, then returned to Fenton. The other straightened up from where he had been leaning nonchalantly against one of the trees and gave him a studying look. 'Well?'

'A smell of smoke, nothin' else.'

'Then he's there?'

'I figure so.'

'What do we do next?' Fenton waited for an answer, stonily patient.

'We'll take him from two sides. That shack he's thrown up won't stand a few shells. Most of the timber is rotten anyway. We pump a few slugs into it. If he comes runnin' we let him have it in the open.'

'And if he doesn't run?'

'Then we just go in and get him.' Tollison swung an arm, indicating the east. 'You go that way. When you're in position, give a whistle. Got that?'

'Sure.' Despite his bland manner, Fenton was a little worried about the situation. The place was too damned quiet and spooky for his liking. He did not feel just as confident as to the outcome of this nocturnal excursion. The shack was all in darkness, it was true – and silent – but Kelsey would be expecting an attack to be made against him, and unless he was a bigger fool than he imagined, he would have taken precautions.

Tollison moved steadily through the brush patch, paused when he reached the end of it, straining his eyes and ears, every nerve and fibre in him tensed so that it hurt. Out of the corner of his eye he watched Fenton, who was almost thirty yards away to the right of him. He could see the branches of the bushes move as the little gunman glided between them, but he knew he would hear no noise. He had heard that Fenton had learned some of his tricks from the Apache.

Crawling along on his belly for six yards, he went down behind the crazily tilted horse trough on the edge of what had once been the courtyard. It lay perhaps fifteen yards from the front of the house and from there it was possible for him to cover both the front and one side. It was up to Fenton to keep an eye on the rest of the place. He eased up the barrel of the Winchester he had brought with him, levelling it on the wall ahead of him, his finger on the trigger, already taking up the slack.

The thin, high-pitched whistle came suddenly from somewhere to the rear of the shack, breaking the clinging stillness. Gently Tollison tightened his finger, curling it about the trigger. If Kelsey hadn't been wakened by that sound, then by God he soon would be. He fired, levered, fired again – five times, laying the pattern of fire along the wall about two feet from the ground level. He heard the splintered crash of the slugs as they ripped into the wood above the shrieking echoes of the shots. From the other side Fenton's answering fire came as he poured a fusillade into the place.

Now we'll see just how good Kelsey is, Merl thought savagely, with a vicious curl of his lips. We'll see how good his nerves are, if he's still alive.

Inside the shack, Dave Kelsey came awake at once at the first crash of gunfire. Every sense instinctively alert, like those of an animal, he rolled swiftly off the low bunk, hit the floor and wriggled on his elbows to the wall immediately beneath the window which looked out on to the courtyard, grabbing at the Colt hanging beside the bunk. More slugs tore through the wall just above his head, slamming across the room and burying themselves deeply in the far wall at his back.

For several moments, he lay quite still, searching around with eyes and ears, trying to pinpoint the direction from which the fire was coming. After a little while, he felt reasonably certain there were only two men out there, one at the front and the other to the rear of the shack. That made things a little more even, but he was pinned down, and the moment he showed himself he was liable to get his head blown off.

I came a damn long way to wind up like a coyote caught in a trap, he thought bitterly.

There came a brief lull in the gunfire. Carefully he lifted his head until his eyes were on a level with the window ledge, peering out into the darkness outside.

He could not see the gunman from there. Maybe back among the brush or even closer, behind the horse trough which alone provided any cover within twenty yards of the front of the building. Bringing up the Colt, he sighted it on the trough, squeezed off a couple of shots. He heard the dull thud of lead hammering into the wood, then caught the sudden instinctive movement as the man behind the trough moved involuntarily.

He caught only a fragmentary glimpse of the dark figure as the other shifted his position slightly, and he could not be certain of his identification in the pale moonlight, but he felt reasonably sure who the other was. Merl Tollison! He studied the terrain thoughtfully. If he tried to make a break from the shack, he would be gunned down for sure before he had gone a couple of paces. From that distance, a man like Merl Tollison could scarcely miss. Yet somehow he had to get out and under cover. He knew the lie of the land here better than either of these two killers. He felt sure that once in the dark shadows, the advantage would pass to him. Perhaps the others were aware of this for at that precise moment both men opened up again, quartering the shack with well-placed shots, designed to force him to keep his head down.

Dave was not in a mood to take chances. He had to match cunning with cunning in a situation like this. Wood splintered within an inch of his head and something nicked his cheek, drawing blood.

'Kelsey!'

Dave glanced up sharply at the unexpected sound of his name. He had not thought the other would give himself away like that.

'We know you're there. Better come on out with your hands lifted.'

Dave waited, thumbed a couple of cartridges into the empty chambers of the Colt. He did not intend to rush into something that could be resolved with patience. Let the silence work on them, he thought grimly. Let them realise that they were wasting their time shooting blind, that they would have to make a fresh move if they wanted to kill him. In his mind's eye, he visualized the lay-out of the ground around the shack. To the front there was scarcely any cover, to the rear lay the ruins of the ranch house. He would have a better chance there than anywhere else.

Carefully he worked his way back across the floor into the half-finished room at the back. Here the wooden boards had not yet been nailed into place and, crouching down, he peered intently through a gap between two of them. He was slightly higher than the position of the unknown killer at the back, but here the mesquite and thorn were dotted thickly over the ground, providing plenty of cover for the gunman. There was no time to waste seeking the other out. Bending, getting his legs under him, he loosed off a couple of shots into the brush, waited for a second. The answering shots came almost at once.

There!

The brief stilettos of orange flame came from a small knoll to his right. The slugs tore wood from the boards as he thrust himself out into the open, raced for the nearest patch of cover, throwing himself down behind it. More slugs kicked up dirt at his heels. Breathing hard, he crawled rapidly on hands and knees for a couple of yards. Now he could hear the other man as he too shifted his position. Boots scraped on rock. He could picture the killer in the brush, straining to see him, not knowing whether his shots had found their mark or not. The moon had now lifted above the trees on the eastern slope, shining balefully into the clearing at the rear of the burnt-out ranch. Dave began to edge forward, his Colt gripped in his right hand, watching the bushes ahead of him, a pale blur in the moonlight. He smiled tightly in the dimness, even though he could feel the tension growing and working through him, knotting the muscles of his stomach. There was more scraping of boots on loose stones. Gravel rattled less than ten yards away.

There was another breathless hush and then the brief stab of muzzle flame, blue-crimson in the darkness. Dave felt the wind of the slug as it hummed through the air close to his head. But the shot had given the other man away. Swiftly, scarcely pausing to think, he rose up on to his knees, saw the man lying flat on his stomach on a narrow shelf of rock, saw the other turn his head, eyes widening as the pale moonlight fell full on the narrow, cruel features. The other tried to swing his gun to bear on him against his wrist. Close on the sharp explosion he fired again, heard the strangled gasp as both slugs tore into the gunman's body, hurling him back to the ground under the shuddering impact of the flying lead.

Fenton went sprawling back, first on to his knees, the Colt dropping from nerveless fingers, then even further back, his spine arching into a fantastic posture, hands clutching at his chest. There was a vague look of stupefied astonishment on his face as he hung there, staring up at Dave, poised above him. Then a long, guttering sigh came from his slack lips, blood gushing down his chin and he flopped loosely sideways, his hat falling off as his head struck the rock hard. He lay still, unmoving.

Carefully, Dave went forward, although he was certain the man had been dead before he hit the dirt. He felt the other's outflung arm, knew by the flaccid limpness that there was no life left in the man. He let go the other's wrist. He did not recognise the man but his face bore the unmistakable stamp of a profession killer. One of Clem Tollison's hired gunslingers, he reckoned.

He paused for only a moment, thumbed fresh shells into the Colt, then drifted into the brush, circling around the shack. Merl Tollison was still out front and if the other should discover that his companion was now dead, that he was alone, fighting on even terms, his first thought would be for his own safety.

Ignoring the sharp, cutting thorns of the bushes, he moved rapidly. As he rounded the edge of the courtyard, he made out the shapes of the two horses, standing a little distance away. Evidently the two men had approached the shack on foot, hoping to make no sound. There was no sign of Tollison. Gun ready, he slid down a shallow bank, eyes alert.

For a moment the silence remained absolute. Then, off to his left, some fifteen yards from the horse trough where Merl had been hiding previously, the other's voice drifted down to him.

'What's goin' on back there, Charlie?'

Dave smiled thinly. The other was still some way from the horses and there was a stretch of open ground he would have to cross to reach them. 'Tollison!' He yelled. 'Better throw up your hands and come on out! Your side-kick is dead. You'll get no help from him.'

The words echoed in the narrowness. Merl Tollison made his decision. Three or four shots ripped from the other's gun so swiftly that they blended into a single roll of sound. But the other was nervous now. This sudden and unexpected turn of events had touched him badly. All of the slugs went wide of where Dave lay.

'You're shootin' wild now, Tollison. What's the matter? Gettin' scared now we're on even terms?'

'I'm goin' to kill you, Kelsey,' called back the other. 'Jeb wanted to do it because of the beatin' up you gave him a few days back, but I figured I'd do it myself.'

Dave slipped through the trees, circled well past the house, came to the thicker, more tangled, growth on the far side of the hill. He reckoned now he was behind the other. Somewhere below, if he had guessed right, Merl Tollison was holed up down there, waiting for him to make a move. Inch by inch he wormed his way forward through the trees, pausing as he heard the faint sound from directly in front of him. The sudden exhalation of pent-up breath gave away Tollison's position. Dave stiffened as he saw the other behind a tall outcrop of rock. For a moment the sharp anger inside him made him want to shoot the other there and then, but some inner sense prompted him to call out: 'Drop your gun, Tollison. Now!'

It was a moment of decision for the other. Dave saw the man stiffen as his words rang out, saw the sudden tensing of the shoulders. Tollison remained staring straight ahead for several seconds, not moving. Then, in a blurring motion, he whirled, throwing himself to one side in the same instant, the gun in his hand flashing flame and smoke as he squeezed off two shots in Dave's direction. Chips of bark flew from the tree within inches of Dave's head as the slugs tore into it.

Dave fired a single shot. The burned powder bloomed crimson in the black night and somewhere in the echoing racket, somewhere in the heart of the sound, he heard Merl Tollison give up a great cry. Then sound and cry faded and there was only the stink of powder in his nostrils and the slowly atrophying echoes chasing themselves across the clearing. Going forward slowly, gun held ready, he heard the other's guttering breath and, coming up to the man, he found him lying with his shoulders against one of the stunted trees. The gun had slipped from his limp fingers, but he was still vainly trying to get his hand around it and lift it once more, face twisted into a spasm of pain and stark disbelief.

His body twisted sharply as agony tore through his chest and a racking cough brought flecks of blood to his lips. 'Goddamn you, Kelsey!' His voice was a snarling whisper. 'The boys will get you for this, I promise you.'

Dave said thinly: 'Reckon you'll be in hell a long time before that happens, Merl. You should have thought of this before you rode with the rest of your family and wiped out mine. Or maybe you figured I wouldn't come back lookin' for vengeance.'

'You'll never settle here. They'll finish you,' said Tollison. He had been slowly stirring against the trees, struggling with a fanatical desperation to force strength into his right hand, but his fingers fell limply to the ground and his breathing was silent. Dave waited for a moment, then touched the other's body with his foot, turning it over. It flopped limply to one side, the humped looseness going fully slack.

For a moment he thought of what had happened here more than a year before, waiting for the sense of fulfilment and satisfaction to come. But, curiously, there was nothing like that. In his body and brain there was only an odd emptiness which he could neither define nor really understand. He had thought he would have felt good now that part of his mission had succeeded and one of the hated Tollisons had paid the supreme price. But instead, he was dry and tired, and there was an unpleasant sensation in his mind which lay beyond every other emotion.

Moving away from the scene, he went back to the shack, threw himself down on the bunk, hands clasped behind his neck. This black mood, this oddly irritable and formless feeling which he could not properly analyse, refused to dissolve and leave him in peace. He felt finished and useless. Maybe if it had been the end of everything, he might have felt better; but unfortunately, as he well knew, this was only the beginning.

Somewhere during the early hours of the morning, long before grey dawn lit the clearing, a faint flurry of sound struck down through the woolly layers of sleep around Dave's brain to reach that part of him which never really slept. It was like the rustle of the wind in the dry leaves of a dead tree or a thickly tangled bunch of mesquite. He heard it as he would a sound in a dream, then it faded and there was nothing more. When he woke, the memory was gone.

His mouth was dry and during the night the norther, which had picked up freshness, had driven the dust in through the cracks in the boards, laying a thin layer of it over everything. He rubbed the back of his hand over his face, felt it scratch his flesh, lay for a moment, back-tracking in his memory. Then he remembered the gunfight during the night – Merl Tollison and that gunhawk who had ridden with him.

What to do with the bodies, still lying out there? If he rode into town with them and reported the incident to the sheriff, the chances were high that he would find himself thrown into jail, and then he would be at the mercy of the rest of the Tollisons. He could visualise what their reaction would be when they heard of the night's happenings.

He pondered the problem while he got his shaving gear, washed and shaved in cold water, using a small mirror balanced against the window. Then he dried himself, went out and stood on the small splintered porch for a moment, watching the first sunlight break the clear morning air. For a moment a little of the good feeling came back as the air went down like wine into his lungs. Only for a moment did it return, then the sight of the sprawled body half-hidden among the bushes in the distance took it away and he knew, even if he had not known before, that it would never be the same again.

Returning to the shack, he ate a couple of strips of jerky beef, chewing them thoughtfully, and washing them down with cold water. Five minutes later he went outside again, walked slowly to where Merl Tollison's body lay. The other was lying flat on his back in the bushes, the middle of his body arched slightly upwards as if, even in death, he was trying to get up and continue to fight. Forcing himself into the brush, he got his hands under the other's armpits and began dragging the dead man out into the open, the dragging spurs carving twin trails in the dirt. He sweated a little over the job, in spite of the coolness of the air at that time of morning.

Straightening up to ease the ache in his shoulders, he dug into his pocket, took out tobacco and paper and rolled himself a cigarette. He was still unsure what to do with the two dead men. They were a problem he had not counted on. Though the first drag of smoke stung the back of his throat, he inhaled it with relish, savouring it slowly. His eyes were pulled back to a deep shadowiness beneath his brows. Better find the two horses, he reflected, maybe he could then—

'Hold it right there, Kelsey!'

Dave stiffened abruptly. He did not recognise the voice, but there was something in it that warned him not to make a try for his gun, that told him there was a weapon laid on his back, ready for any move like that.

'That's better.' Someone stepped up behind him, slipped the Colt from its holster and tossed it away into the mesquite. 'Now turn around.'

Slowly Dave did as he was told. The man who stood behind him wore a star on his shirt and the gun in his right hand was pointed directly at Dave's middle. Ben Chapman. A bunch of men stood a little distance away, watching.

'Vince,' Chapman called without turning his head. 'Get over here and take a look. See how Merl was killed.'

One of the men moved away from the group, went down on one knee beside Tollison, rolled him over, then looked up. 'Right through the heart,' he said woodenly. 'Ain't no doubt about it, Sheriff.'

Chapman smiled thinly. 'That's what I figured. Scout around. See if you can find any sign of Charlie Fenton. He rode out with Merl. Bound to be around here some place.'

'He's back of the shack, in the trees,' Dave said tightly. Thinning his lips, he went on. 'Don't get any fool ideas about this, Sheriff. These two hombres sneaked up on me durin' the night, ambushed me in the shack and did their level best to murder me.'

'So you tell me,' muttered Chapman. 'Reckon we only have your word for that. It's damned certain neither of these men can testify against you.'

Dave glanced over the other's shoulder, looked at the rest of the men in the posse. He saw taut accusation on their faces. 'What do you call it then, Chapman,' he snapped, 'when two men get into a gunfight with one? I didn't invite 'em out here, and you can see for yourselves neither of 'em was shot in the back, so there was no bushwhack.'

'What the hell does that matter?' flared Chapman. 'We all know of the feud between you and the Tollisons.' There was a grin that was partly an incredulous sneer on the lawman's face. 'You came here lookin' for trouble and, by golly, you sure found it – big trouble.' He glanced round as the man called Vince came back into the small clearing.

'He's there all right,' grunted the other. 'Shot just like Merl.' There was a puzzled look on his features. 'Charlie Fenton was one of the fastest guns in the business. Reckon there ain't a man in the territory could outdraw or outshoot him in even fight.'

'He had his gun in his hand when I called him,' Dave said flatly. 'I know this land better than they did. I could've come up on 'em from behind and shot 'em in the back without warnin' even after they'd got me in the shack.'

'You're trying to say they rode in and penned you down in the shack and you managed to get out and kill 'em both?' Chapman's voice was as thin and cold as a sliver of ice.

''I'm sayin' just that.'

The lawman shrugged. 'You'll get a chance to tell that to a jury soon as the circuit judge gets here. In the meantime, I'm takin' you back into town.' There was a curious expression at the back of his deep-sunk eyes; almost one of awe. 'Guess this is for your own protection, Kelsey. Maybe it did happen the way you say, but that ain't how Old Man Tollison is goin' to see it when he hears of this. You'll be safer in jail until you get a trial than you will be out here. Now get your mount and saddle up.' He turned his head slowly to the other men. 'A couple of you boys get these bodies on to their horses.'

Fifteen minutes later they rode out of the clearing, the dead men slung over the saddles of their mounts, Dave riding between two men, his hands tied behind his back. It was difficult for him to keep his balance in the saddle, and as the sun lifted and the heat grew more intense, every movement of his mount on the rough trail jarred through his body. They rode in silence, each man engrossed in his own thoughts. Out of the corner of his eyes, Dave studied the men who rode with Chapman. Some of these men, he reflected bitterly, had known his father, had known him to be a straight and honest man. Yet here they were, taking him as a prisoner, either believing all of the lies or because they dare do nothing else.

Turning his head a little, he eyed Chapman. The sheriff rode tall in the saddle, keeping his gaze fixed straight ahead of him, not once turning to look at him. How much could the lawman be trusted to get him a fair trial? He pondered. Maybe even at the end of this little charade, all he would get would be a small lump of lead, maybe the Tollisons were at the back of this, simply using Chapman to do their dirty work for them, not wanting the townsfolk to know their true worth.

As he rode he tested the knots, tensing and slackening his wrists alternately. But those knots had been well tied, would never be loosened. He forced himself to relax, thought once more about Chapman. The sheriff was, as Stacy Herbison had truly said, a weak man. He was a tool in the hands of the Tollisons, weak perhaps, but at the moment more than necessary. As yet he guessed they could not come out into the open. But what Chapman did not realise was that once the tool had served its purpose, it would be utterly discarded. Old Clem Tollison would see to it that there would be no wealth or power for a man like Ben Chapman. No doubt the other was already dreaming of holding some important position in the territory once Tollison had got all he wanted. If that was the case, then he would be doomed to disappointment. Tollison would kill him as soon as his usefulness was finished.

Three hours later, with the sunlight throwing a blistering net on to the streets and alleys and the buildings with their peeling paint hanging off the walls in thin strips, they rode into town. Chapman was visibly pale and tensed as he looked about him, eyeing the boardwalk and the land agency with Clem Tollison's name on the window in particular, with a nervous look. A few loafers drifted over to the edge of the boardwalk, moving out of the cooler shadows to watch the small party as they reined up in front of the jail.

'Jack and Peter,' said Chapman sharply. 'Take the bodies along to the morgue. Then get yourselves a drink at the saloon. It's been a long and thirsty ride.'

The lawman waited until the two men had ridden off around a corner of the street, then looked bleakly at Dave.

'Get down, Kelsey,' he said thinly. 'Don't give me any trouble or I might alter my decision and turn you over to Old Man Tollison right now.'

Hooking his leg over the saddle, Dave dropped to the dusty street, jerked himself back on balance, leaning for a moment against his horse's flank to steady himself. Chapman dismounted, pulled his gun and prodded him into the building. Over his shoulder the sheriff called: 'That's all for now, boys.'

Inside the office, Dave said: 'Do you have to keep my wrists tied, Chapman?'

'Just a precaution, Kelsey,' said the other tartly. 'If you're as dangerous as they say you are, then I don't intend takin' any chances.'

Dave looked at him closely. 'Then you do believe that I shot those men in fair fight.'

Chapman shrugged his shoulders. 'Ain't no concern of mine how it happened,' he muttered. 'My job is just to bring you in. The charge against you will still be murder, whatever you say to me. When they try you, it'll be up to you to defend yourself. If the jury believe you, then I reckon you'll go free.'

Dave's lips curled into a contemptuous grin. 'You reckon I'll get a fair trial, with the Tollisons runnin' this whole town, Chapman? There ain't a man in Big Stone Gap or within twenty miles of it who'd find me not guilty.

You know that as well as I do.'

'Reckon you should have foreseen somethin' like this when you rode into town and decided to stay,' muttered the other. He took down a bunch of keys from the wall behind his desk, nodded his head towards the door on the far side of the room. 'The rope comes off your wrists when you're inside the cell. Not before.'

North of the James River – beyond Roanoke and Lynchburg – days to the north of Big Stone Gap but swinging steadily south over the wide plains and the cedar forests, through the narrow gaps in the hills, come five men. Grim-faced men, lean and sharp-eyed. Men who carried their guns slung low on their hips, faces tanned a deep brown to the texture of old leather. Fast men with a gun who had agreed to follow the small, ferret-faced man who led them.

Frenchy LaVere, bent on vengeance, was heading south, working his way along the trail taken by Dave Kelsey some weeks before. They rode hard, stopped only here and there to ask discreet questions, to check they were still on the right trail. Mile on mile they drew closer to Big Stone Gap.

There was one night high on the bluffs some seventy miles north-east of the Tennesse border, when the five men sat huddled around a blazing fire on the banks of a small creek that flowed down from the looming heights of the Alleghenies, seeking shelter from the biting wind which shrieked through the trees.

'You sure we're goin' to find this hombre you're ridin' after, Frenchy?' Saul Mureau, out of Texas, far to the west, stared at the other across the leaping flames. 'Seems to me he could be anywhere along this trail. We could even have passed him by in any of those towns to the north.'

'We'll catch up with him,' said the other viciously. 'Those we've asked all said two men rode through a couple of weeks ago. Men whose description fits this coyote and Marengo. I'll find them and I'll kill them.'

Mureau fell silent. All the way from Clayton he had tried to figure out this man who led them on his mission of revenge, but with little success. Crook, gambler, killer, mean, with a temper that flared up viciously at the slightest chance, getting to know him was virtually impossible, and he was not the sort of man one pressed with questions.

Night after night, when the fire died down to a faint glow among the embers, LaVere would go off by himself into the shadows that ringed the camp around, practising his right hand draw with an empty gun, going at it endlessly, continuing it for an hour or more, before he would return, slip into his blanket and sleep.

They ate the thin strips of bacon, fried to a frazzle over the fire, munched on the hard corn bread, washing the unappetising food down with scalding coffee. One by one they moved away from the fire, got into their blankets, shoulders resting in the half-round of upturned saddles, almost too tired to sleep, bitterly cold on that side of their bodies which faced the inrushing wind, warm on the other. There was no surfeit of comfort on this trip, Mureau reflected wearily as he shifted his body, striving to find a more comfortable position on the hard ground.

He stared up at the clear, star-bright heavens, turning his thoughts over in his mind. He was not a man given to apprehensive fear but he could not help wondering what kind of man this Kelsey was who had bested Frenchy LaVere in Clayton, who had earned the other's undying hatred. There would be hell busting loose all over if they finally did meet up with this hombre, he decided.

The movement on the far edge of the fireglow brought his head around. Frenchy got lithely to his feet, stared around at the men in their blankets, then moved silently out of sight into the trees. A few moments later there came the steady, unmistakable click of a hammer on an empty chamber, the sound repeated again and again and again.

Mureau sighed, turned over on to his back, looked up

at the stars. He had known nights like this in those days when he had ridden with Quantrill's raiders, sweeping down on unprotected and unsuspecting towns, leaving them looted and in flames. He felt a certain nostalgia as he allowed the memories to flood back into his tired mind. There had been something about those days, some kind of excitement which had been lacking once the war was finished. Those who rode with Quantrill were outlawed, classed as criminals, hunted down like animals if they failed to give themselves up during the brief amnesty. He had surrendered himself to the Union forces within the specified time, expecting imprisonment, had been mildly surprised when his rifle had been taken from him and he had been turned loose. It was then that his contempt for authority had begun and had grown over the months.

He had drifted from one place to another in the days which had followed, had worked for a month on a ranch, rounding up strays and herding them to the railroad. But the old desires for action had proved stronger than anything else and he had fallen in readily with Frenchy LaVere. At least, with the other he would get action of the kind he had known during the war.

Mureau was still awake when LaVere came back, thrusting the Colt into its holster. The Frenchman tossed a handful of logs on to the fire, sending the flame and sparks leaping high, then settled down in his own blankets. Yawning, Mureau closed his eyes, still wondering about LaVere and Kelsey while he waited for sleep to come.

In the morning they ate a quick meal, saddled their mounts and rode down into the long valley that stretched south along the eastern boundary of the Alleghenies where the mountain chain curved south and west. They stayed with the main trail downward and it took them presently to one of the many narrow canyons which cut diagonally across the foothills. Here the trail continued upward again, heading for a narrow pass high among the rearing ridges, but LaVere swung them off the trail at this point, aside into the thick timber, continuing to parallel the mountains.

He knew none of this land and yet he felt no real concern. Most of his life had been a pattern of hills and valleys such as this and the driving force of his vengeance overrode all other considerations.

5

Dark
Vengeance

With some food inside him, a cigarette between his lips, Dave felt a little better as he sat on the edge of the low bunk. The chafing pain in his wrists had eased, giving him a chance to think clearly, but there seemed to be little profit or advantage in his thinking. He stared through the drifting blue smoke at the small square window, barred with iron, through which he could just see the sky and hear the sounds of the town outside.

Bitterly he could only sit and reflect on the way in which the dice had fallen against him. There was now an inevitability about it which was almost frightening. His one hope now was Ricardo Marengo. But where was the Mexican? Close at hand, or hundreds of miles to the south? Maybe the other had forgotten his promise of help. Things such as these were easily put out of one's mind after only a few short days.

Getting to his feet, he moved across to the door, iron-barred in its upper half, blocked by thick, heavy timber below. Here and there it had been gouged and scored by kicking boots. Grasping the bars in both hands, he pressed his face against them, stared along the short passage.

There was the low murmur of voices from the outer office where Chapman and a couple of his deputies were closeted together. A chair scraped back and there was the scratch of a match, then the yellow glare of lantern light showing beneath the door. Outside there was the gathering gloom of dusk.

Chapman's measured tones echoed along the corridor, but it was impossible to make out any of the words. Dave remained at the cell door for several minutes and then tossed his cigarette butt on to the earth floor, grinding it out under his heel.

As he turned away, the office door opened and in the shaft of yellow light Chapman's broad figure appeared. He shuffled slowly towards the cell.

'You finished with the tray, Kelsey?'

'Reckon so.'

Chapman remained outside the cell, motioned with his hand. 'Then pass it through.' He waited until Dave had pushed the empty tray through the bars.

'Reckon by now the whole town knows I'm locked in here, Chapman.'

'So?'

'What's to stop the Tollisons from ridin' in and bustin' me out of jail?'

'Ain't much, I guess,' mused the others thoughtfully. 'Reckon you'd better start sayin' a few prayers if you know any.'

'You're just as bad as the rest of 'em,' Dave said in a tone of disgust. He turned away and stretched himself out on the bunk, seemingly ignoring the other. After a few moments Chapman turned on his heel and went away.

Before he dropped off Dave thought he heard movement outside, somewhere along the street; a sound like a group of riders moving in slowly, walking their mounts as if anxious not to make too much noise. He strained his ears for a long moment, listening intently; then when nothing happened, he lay back, closed his eyes and went to sleep.

He did not sleep soundly. Perhaps it was the unaccustomed hardness of the bunk, or the half-formed thoughts and ideas which persisted in invading his mind. He woke continually, breathing heavily, his wrists aching where the thongs had bitten tightly into the flesh. There was a dull aching pain in his head that bothered him more and more.

The fourth or fifth time he wakened he had been sleeping a little more soundly than before and, for this reason, instinct warned him that whatever it was that had wakened him, it was more than just a faint sound drifting down into his subconsciousness. It was undeniable something else. He lay under the thin, rough blanket, staring up into the clinging darkness of the cell, letting his eyes become accustomed to the gloom. He could just make out the barred window, a fainter shadow against the black, anonymous background of the wall. A single star gleamed fitfully against the sable of the night.

Carefully, making no sound, he eased himself off the bunk, moved over to the window, standing on the end of the bunk, raising himself as far as possible until he was able to peer through the window. For a long moment it seemed that the narrow alley outside was empty and deserted. Then there was movement, cautious and furtive. He saw the two men move from the concealing shadow of an adobe hut less than thirty yards away, move across the end of the alley in a half-crouch, clearly working their way around into the main street towards the front of the jail.

Dave heard a horse stamp outside some distance away, but close enough to be connected with the men he had seen. Swiftly he moved to the door of the cell, waited, every muscle and fibre in him posed and tensed. For a long moment there was silence, deep and absolute. Then he heard a faint sound in the outer office, like a gentle rapping on the street door, followed by a short, muted conversation. The murmur of voices was not repeated, but almost at once Dave heard the muffled crash as if a heavy body had fallen against a chair.

Seconds later, the connecting door was thrown open. Silhouetted against the pale yellow glow of lamplight, Dave saw the three shadowy figures that came along the corridor. In the dimness he strained to make out who they were, then saw that all three were hooded. With an effort he fought down the sense of alarm that rose within him.

The leading man held the bunch of keys in his hand. Stepping forward, he tried several in the lock before he found the one which fitted. Opening the cell door, he signalled Dave outside.

'Just what is this?' Dave asked harshly. 'Is this the brand of justice they deal out now in Big Stone Gap?'

'Keep your voice down, Kelsey,' said the man in a muffled tone. 'We aim to get you out of here. But we don't want the whole town warned.'

'Just who the hell are you men? And why this interest in freein' me?' Dave demanded.

'Let's just say that we don't like to see a man strung up for somethin' he didn't do,' said the second man in a sibilant hiss. 'Now just move on out of here. Once you're out of town, you can keep ridin' if you've a mind to.'

Dave hesitated. There was something here which didn't quite add up, but he shrugged the idea away. In spite of the hoods they wore, he felt certain that none of these men were the Tollisons. Besides, if he knew Old Clem Tollison, he would just ride on into town any time he had a mind to and break him out of jail with both the sheriff and all of the townsfolk looking on, confident that there would be nobody around who would dare to stop him. It was extremely unlikely he would come in the middle of the night.

Still puzzled, Dave walked in front of the three men into the outer office. In the lamplight he noticed the sprawled figure of the night deputy lying on the floor beside the desk. The big man beside Dave noticed his glance. He said curtly: 'He'll wake up in the mornin' with nothin' worse than a headache. By that time you should be well away from here.'

There was a cool breeze blowing when they emerged into the street. Dave noticed two more men waiting with the horses on the far side of the road, a little way beyond the saloon.

'Mount up, Kelsey,' order the big man tautly. 'Let's get out of here before somebody decides to come a-lookin'.'

Swinging himself up into the saddle, Dave turned the high collar of his jacket up against the wind. He ran a cold glance over the men around him. Were these solid citizens of Big Stone Gap, determined not to allow an injustice to be done, afraid of showing their faces for fear that word of their work this night might come to the ears of the Tollisons. Or was there some deeper and more sinister reason behind the wearing of these hoods for this nocturnal mission? Whatever the answer, he knew that he was, at that moment, in no position to argue about it. Even if they were some of Tollison's men, this escape from jail offered him a chance, a slim one, but still a chance to make a break for it if an opportunity presented itself. One thing was sure. Back there in that cell his chances of escaping a noose were virtually non-existent. At least, now he was out of the confines of those four walls. Not to go with these men would mean being taken back to an inevitable death at the end of a rope.

They walked their horses to the outskirts of town, then raked spurs along the animals' flanks, heading out towards the brush country. Silence fell over the riders. The foothills and the brush country loomed darkly around them. Presently the tall man who appeared to be the leader swung his mount off the trail, led the way down a long inclined wrinkle of ground formed in some past geological age, the tumbled boulders making it impossible for two men to ride abreast.

Dave's nerves had become taut. He knew that, from the attitude of the men in front and behind him, he would be

shot if he tried to make a break for it, and the feeling that
he was being led into a trap became stronger with every
passing second. If these were some of Tollison's men, then
the odds were heavily against him getting more than a few
yards from this bunch.

'You boys intend to ride all the way with me?' He
inquired evenly.

For a moment nobody spoke. Then the man in the lead
turned his head, said softly: 'We figured we'd ride a little
way with you, Kelsey. Just to make sure you got well clear
of town without any trouble.' There was something in the
other's tone, muffled as it was by the thick cowl, that crys-
tallised Dave's suspicions into near certainty.

They rode slowly along the narrow game trail until
eventually it widened out and the open, flat brush country
came into view, spiked here and there by prickly thorn and
cactus. As they rode, Dave's eyes kept flicking from right to
left, looking for a likely spot where it might just be possible for him to make a break for it in the darkness. The trail
ran beside a steeply rising slope, rugged rocks showing
vaguely through the dense chapparal. Fifty yards or so
further on there was a wide gap in the rock wall, sufficiently wide for a horse to pass through with relative ease.
Gripping the reins tightly, Dave waited. There were two
men riding behind him, the others bunched tightly
together in front. None of the men had their hands near
their guns.

As he drew level with the gap Dave deliberately slowed
his mount so that the men ahead of him drew further
away. He heard a muffled curse from one of the men
behind him, twisted in his saddle, turning his head, as if to
say something then rammed his spurs into the horse's
barrel. The animal uttered a shrill whinny of pain as, at
the same time, he pulled hard on the reins, jerking its
head around, sending it leaping for the gap. Behind him
he heard someone utter a startled yell of fury. Then the
out-thrusting rocks were scraping along his legs as he

clung hard into the saddle, bending low over his horse's neck, presenting a more difficult target.

A malignant strand of thorn snaking out of the rocks struck him across the face, drawing blood. Another hit the shoulder, almost throwing him from the saddle. He held on grimly, knowing that he had only a few moments before the others were through that narrow gap, and on his heels. He tried to bend lower in the saddle, but the mesquite that raked the animal's flanks beat savagely at his face, virtually blinding him. Ahead he made out a thick clump of chapparal. Gritting his teeth, he covered his head with one arm as the horse plunged wildly into it. Snorting, tossing its head high, the bay hammered its way through it. Gasping for breath, blood flowing into his eyes from a long gaping gash on his forehead, he straightened up instinctively in the saddle, was forced to duck again a few moments later as an overhanging branch loomed up from nowhere and threatened to unseat him. Now there was nothing he could do but try to dodge the thick clusters of Spanish Sword which could cut a horse's legs to ribbons within seconds. Reeling sideways in the saddle, he listened for any sound of his pursuers, heard them as they came blundering through the gap. They seemed to have lost precious moments in coming after him and he guessed that in their desperate anxiety to recapture him several of them had tried to get through at once.

Gritting his teeth, he forced his mount to continue its headlong flight. Then, without warning, a thick branch reaching across the trail found its mark at last and struck him squarely in the chest, smashing him from the saddle, hurling him into the tangled brush beside the trail.

All of the wind knocked from his lungs, he lay there, utterly unable to move. The incessant pounding of his fear-crazed horse died away but the thunder of other hoof-beats took their place as the men came riding up. He lay quite still, gasping air into his tortured lungs, struggling desperately to keep a tight hold of his consciousness.

Through blurred vision, he saw the head of a rider only a few yards away, silhouetted against the sky. It was the big man. For a moment the other remained there, waiting on the rest of the men. Would they follow the horse in its headlong flight, or would they begin searching for him? The answer came a few moments later. Spreading out, the riders commenced a slow forward movement, sweeping the thick brush. He tried to blend himself into the contours of the ground, rolled sideways into thorn that tore at his flesh and clothing.

The end came suddenly. Drawing in his legs, Dave tried to crawl into a narrow opening which led deeper into the scrub. Then steel-shod hooves crashed on an outcrop of rock, a man gave vent to a sudden yell and the snaking loop of a riata caught Dave around the legs, drawing abruptly tight, hauling him out into the open. The uneven ground rubbed his back and shoulders raw, tearing his flesh. His jacket had been ripped and torn in several places and there was very little of his shirt and vest left, and what little there was had been reduced to rags and tatters.

'It was a damned good try, Kelsey,' snarled the big man, thinly. 'But not just good enough.'

The rest of the men laughed. Dave struggled into a sitting position. Each movement brought a fresh rush of pain into the upper half of his body. One of the men got down from his mount, came forward to loosen the riata from around his legs.

'Reckon it would serve you right if we was to drag you the rest of the way along the ground for that trick you just played,' he grunted. Jerking the rope free, he hauled Dave roughly to his feet. Swaying drunkenly on legs that seemed scarcely able to bear his weight, he drew in a great gust of air, winced at the agony which lanced through his chest. As he stood there, he was aware that the others had pulled off the black hoods. Blinking rapidly, he stared at them. He did not recognise a single man, but it was easy to guess the kind of men they were. Killer breed. He knew now with a sick certainty that they were not citizens of Big Stone Gap.

The big man had pale eyes and drooping moustache. His eyes were set close together, mouth twitching slightly all the time as if there was some nerve there that gave him no rest.

'All right,' he said, his voice thin and weak. 'The little game is over. Maybe you'll tell me what all this is about. Why you went to all of this trouble to break me out of jail. Seems to me I haven't met any of you men before.'

The others grinned. 'Hear that, boys?' He turned to glance at the others. 'Kelsey wants to know why we took all this trouble to free him?'

The man coiling the riata looked up. 'Let's say there's somebody who's mighty anxious to make your acquaintance.'

'Tollison?' Dave spoke the name harshly. He rubbed the back of his hand across his mouth.

'Now you're gettin' clever,' nodded the other. He tied the rope on to his saddle.

The big man said: 'He can ride up with you, Finn. It's only a matter of a couple of miles now. Then we can turn him over to Tollison.'

In the cold grey light of a chilly dawn, the party rode towards a stand of pin-oak on a small ridge. Dave let his glance wander over the hummocky country about him. It was many years since he had ridden this way, but various details were familiar to him. Over the ridge stretched empty desert for close on twenty miles or so before it passed into Tennessee. It was bad country. Bare rocks and white powder-alkali with a few water holes at this dry season. Doubt moved in him as he eyed the trees ahead. If the Tollisons were waiting here, why had they chosen this out-of-the-way place to get rid of him when they could do it in far greater safety on their own place?

Shivering as the cold morning air struck through the holes in his jacket, touching his flayed back with a burning sensation. Fifteen yards from the stand of pin-oak, the big man reined up his mount, lifted his right hand in a signal to halt.

'You sure this is the place, Curly?' asked Finn, leaning forward a little in the saddle.

'Sure. Here they are now,' answered the other.

Even as he spoke, three riders spurred their mounts out of the trees, moved towards them. Dave narrowed his eyes as he recognised the men. Old Man Tollison, flanked by Creede and Jeb. There were no words from the men around Dave. No sound. No movement by riders nor the horses on which they sat. It was as if they all sensed death in the air. Now Clem Tollison reined up his mount directly in front of the men. His head came up, eyes staring directly at Dave. For a long moment there seemed to be no expression whatsoever on his face.

Then his lips twisted into a vicious look. A rasping breath was drawn deep into his flaring nostrils.

'You killed Merl.' It was simply said, but each word carried the conviction of death. Cold rage worked itself on his features, showed in the deep-set eyes. 'For that, if for nothing else, I'm going to have you killed, Kelsey.'

'Aren't you forgettin' that you murdered my family, shot them down in cold blood?'

'You killed Merl,' repeated the other flatly. His lips, stretched across his teeth, seemed set into some kind of bestial snarl. His voice was soft and penetrating with something of a snake-hiss in it. 'Now you can get down off that horse.' The bright eyes remained glazed specks.

'You promised I'd get the chance at him,' broke in Jeb Tollison thickly. 'After what he did to me in the saloon, it's only right that—'

'That was before he shot Merl,' said the older man tightly. 'I'm running' this show now. I've got my own ideas about the way he's goin' to die, and it won't be quick.

Before the end he'll be yellin' and screamin' for somebody to put a bullet into him and end his misery.'

Dave hesitated, looked about him swiftly. But there was
no chance at all of escape here. If he tried to make a move,
he would be shot in the leg, anywhere to incapacitate him
but not kill him. Swinging a leg over the horse's rump, he
dropped to the ground, forcing himself to stand upright.
The deadly precariousness of his position washed over
him like a sickness, and he now began to see the plot
which had been in Tollison's brain.

Sitting tall in the saddle, Clem Tollison let his glance
move over the men who had brought Dave there. He
nodded swiftly. 'All right, boys. You can high-tail it back to
the ranch. Reckon we can handle things now.'

Dave rubbed the palms of his hands along his pants
legs, flexed his numbed fingers. 'You can't pull it off,
Tollison. Too many people know about this.'

'I don't want to hear any talk from you. Talk doesn't
worry me in the least. No matter what folk may think,
there'll be no way of provin' anything.'

'And if some of these men start talkin' in the saloon in
town?' Dave jerked his head in the direction of the men
spurring their mounts away to the north-east.

The other shook his head. 'They won't talk,' he said
with conviction. 'And it won't be botherin' *you* even if they
do.'

Tollison waited until the riders were out of sight and
only the faint dust cloud hung unmoving in the air. Then
he pointed off to the south, towards the desert beyond the
pin-oaks. 'Now get movin'. You've got a long way to walk.'

Dave ascended the low rise, stumbled through the oaks,
with the three riders following. Half an hour later the sun
lifted clear of the eastern horizon and the early morning
chill gave way to an increasing warmth. Out here the country was only sparsely populated with stunted growths and
occasional pillars of sagpno cactus. Dave was sweating
profusely even with only the rags of his shirt and vest hang-

ing on his back. Dried blood had crusted over the deep
abrasions in his flesh and his mouth sagged open as his
chest heaved and wheezed with his breathing. Behind him
the three riders were watchful, their hands never straying
from the guns at their hips. It seemed the journey was to
be endless. Ahead of them stretched nothing but the flat,
virtually featureless expanse of the Badlands. As yet he had
no idea of what Tollison had in mind for him, although
more and more it was beginning to look as if the other
intended leaving him out here in the middle of the desert
to die of thirst.

Stumbling, he edged his way up a rising slope, feet sliding in the treacherous loose alkali. At the top he paused,
looked back.

'All right, Kelsey. This is far enough.' Clem Tollison had
his Colt out, the weapon levelled on Dave's chest.

'If you intend shootin' me, reckon you'd better get it
over with right now,' Dave gritted harshly. He glared at the
other through slitted eyes. 'Because if you make a mistake,
I'll come back for you. Guess you know that, don't you,
Tollison?'

The other smiled. There was no mirth in the thin
twitching of the man's lips. The deep-set eyes glared with
an inner fire. 'I don't aim to shoot you, Kelsey, like you did
Merl. It's goin' to be a slow roastin' in hell as far as you're
concerned. I promised you that before you died you'll be
yellin' for a bullet to put an end to your sufferings. I never
go back on my word.'

He turned his head slightly. 'Creede! You got the shovel
and the irons ready?'

The older man nodded briefly as if the proceedings no
longer interested him. Sharply, he said: 'All right, Kelsey.
Start digging. Jeb – find a stake. A strong one.'

Reluctantly the other got down, moved off along the
scrub oaks and cacti. Clem Tollison said thinly: 'Dig yourself a hole, Kelsey. One big enough for the stake Jeb's gone
to find. Guess you can figure it out now. I'm goin' to drive

that stake hard into the ground, pack it real tight so you won't have a chance of movin' it. Then I'm fixin' to chain you to it by the foot. After that, me and the boys are going to ride on out of here.' He lifted his head and threw a quick glance at the cloudless heavens. 'Reckon it won't be long before the buzzards get here. Strange how they can always scent death even when it's quite a ways off.' He grinned viciously. 'After that, it's up to you. Either you lie here and die of thirst, or you get so goddamn weak that the buzzards take you whether you're dead or not. Or' – he paused significantly – 'if you care to lose a foot maybe you'll make it away from here. Either way, you won't stay on my back like you have these past few days, and I reckon Merl will sleep a little sounder in his grave.'

'If it's of any interest to you, Tollison, pretty soon you'll all be swingin' on the end of a rope. That Mexican hombre who rode into town with me. Happened to be a good friend of mine. A few more days and he'll come ridin' back lookin' for me, and he'll have fifty or more men with him. If he should ride in and not find me, he's got word to ride straight for your place and burn it to the ground and hang you for the killers you are.'

For just a moment the other showed some concern. It was clear that he already knew about Morengo and he was just a little unsure of how much Dave was now telling him was the truth and how much was pure bluff. Finally he shrugged it away. 'If they try anythin', I'm sure we know how to take care of them,' he said sharply. 'Besides, the townsfolk aren't too kindly disposed to Mexicans. Had too much trouble with 'em in the past. I've no doubt I can rely on them to back me against these friends of yours. Always assumin' that they turn up. Now move lively and get that hole dug. Any funny business and Creede here will put a bullet into your foot, smashing your ankle into a dozen pieces.'

Dave braced the edge of the shovel against the alkali, thrust deeply into it, shovelling it on one side. It was not difficult work. The ground was soft and powdery, but simply because of its nature it kept flowing back into the hole as he tried to deepen and enlarge it, the edges crumbling inward under the weight of his own boots around it. Gradually, however, the hole deepened. The stinging dust caught at the back of his throat, filled his mouth, burned his eyes and formed a white, irritating mask on his sweating face. He worked slowly, playing for time, until Creede pulled the Winchester from its scabbard and levelled it ominously on him, warning him to speed things up.

Three feet down the edge of the shovel struck something hard and unyielding. The scrape of it carried to the watching men. Jeb came forward, motioned Dave away from the hole and peered in.

'He's hit rock,' he called. 'Reckon this will be good enough.'

'All right.' Clem Tollison stepped down from his horse, wiping the film of sweat from his face with a red bandanna. 'Now hammer that stake in and make damned sure it's good and firm.'

Dave sucked in a sharp breath. As Jeb placed the stake in position and hammered it home, he told himself that once he was chained to it, there would be no hope for him at all. Here, they were several miles off any of the trails and nobody came this way from one end of the year to the other. Even if, by some miracle, he succeeded in freeing himself, he could not hope to make it back on foot. Out of his dust-blurred vision, he measured the distance to Jeb Tollison. The spade he held would make an extremely potent club, but his aim would have to be fast and sure, and even then he could only take one of them with him because long before he could get close enough to the others, they would shoot him down. But Jeb motioned him away from the hole, keeping him at a safe distance.

Ten minutes later, with the sand and alkali packed tightly around the half buried stake, Jeb stepped back. He tested it with his weight, grunting with the strain as he struggled to push and pull it out of the ground, but it had been deeply set and did not budge an inch. Satisfied, he nodded up at his father.

'Guess he'll never shift that,' he muttered.

'Good. Then get the chains on him and let's get out of here. Another hour and that sun is goin' to make it hotter than the hinges of hell.'

Dave tensed himself as Creede got down from his mount, dragging the length of heavy chain after him. It was the sort of thing men used on steers and bulls, Dave noticed absently, tightening his grip on the handle of the shovel. Two rings at the end, broad-banded, for locking by the padlocks around an animal's foot. Crude, but deadly effective.

Creede moved in. When he was less than five feet away there came the booming rocket of a gunshot. The slug ploughed up the sand within a couple of inches of Dave's foot. The sharp crack sent a race of echoes bouncing over the desert. Jumping back instinctively, Dave tripped and fell, the shovel flying from his grasp.

'That's just in case you got any funny ideas about the shovel you were holdin',' said Clem Tollison thinly. 'As you'll see, there ain't nothing wrong with my marksmanship.'

Creede moved up to him warily, eyes alert for the first false move. 'Don't be plannin' nothing unless you want a smashed ankle,' he said, grinning. Thinning his lips, he went on, 'I'm going to enjoy doin' this, Kelsey. Pity I can't stick around and watch you die slowly. Maybe you'll go mad before that happens. Gets real hot out here in the desert around high noon, and they do say the heat can do strange things to a man's mind. Still, I'll be with you in spirit if not in the flesh.'

'You're sure goin' to roast in hell for a long time,' gritted Dave. He tried to struggle up into a standing position, tensing his legs under him, determined to make a try for it, even with that gun levelled on him. Even a bullet in the

chest would be preferable to dying slowly of thirst out here
in the Badlands.

Jerking himself forward, his hands outstretched for the
shovel lying a few feet away, he swung in under the other's
arms, hoping to put Creede between himself and Clem's
gun. In this he succeeded. He heard the old man yell at
Creede to get out of the way, the other unable to fire for
fear of hitting his son. But he had reckoned without
Creede. Almost as if he had been waiting for his move, had
indeed been hoping Dave would try something, the other
jerked himself back a little way, swung the chain, heavily
weighted at the end by the broad iron hoop. Twenty
pounds of metal struck Dave solidly on the side of the
head. Lights flashed momentarily in front of his vision, but
he was unconscious before his body toppled and hit the
ground.

It was close on high noon, with the zenith-high sun beating down on all sides from the inverted furnace bowl of
the steel-blue heavens, when the small group of riders
rode into the outskirts of Big Stone Gap. To Frenchy
LaVere, the place was no different to a hundred others he
had visited in his lifetime, no better and no worse. But if
the information he had been given along the trail to the
north-east was anywhere close to the truth, it had one
different aspect about it which made it important to him.
It was Dave Kelsey's home town. If he was to run the other
to earth any place, it was most likely to be here.

He glanced about him as he walked his horse forward
along the exact middle of the wide dusty street. The white
façade of a church showed on his left, set back from the
main street as if those who had built it had not wanted it
continually in sight. Further along, where the street
widened a little into a square, there was a solitary wide-
trunked tree, throwing a welcome shade in the blistering
heat for the small knot of men seated on the round bench
beneath it.

The eastbound stage was just swinging away from in front of the depot as the men reined up in front of the sheriff's office. Stepping down, Frenchy looped the reins over the hitching rail, glanced up at the other men. 'Grab yourselves a drink and get a bite to eat, boys,' he said genially. 'Reckon this is goin' to take a little time and we'll have to play our hand carefully.'

He waited on the boardwalk until the others had drifted over to the saloon then pushed open the door of the office and stepped inside. There were two men in the office. One whom he took to be the sheriff was seated behind the massive oak desk with his feet up, his hat tilted down over his eyes, his pudgy hands clasped over his stomach. The other, with a bandage wound around his head, was stacking rifles along the far wall.

Frenchy paused in the front of the desk, saw the man at the wall turn to look at him with a quickening interest, then glance away again. Frenchy waited for a brief moment, then reached forward, caught the other's right ankle in a grip of steel and heaved the man's legs to one side so that they slithered across the desk and crashed on to the floor, jerking the lawman from his chair.

The other made a quick grab for his gun, then paused with his hand in mid-air as he caught a glimpse of the expression on Frenchy's face. Thinking better of it, he lowered his hand, an angry flush spreading up from his neck.

'All right, mister,' he growled. 'What is all this about? Who are you to come bustin' in here when I'm takin' a siesta?'

'I take it that you're the sheriff in this town?'

'You take it right,' grunted Chapman. 'Now what's on your mind? And it had better be good.'

'I'm looking for a man,' LaVere said flatly. 'I've reason to believe he's here in this town.'

'So you're looking for a man,' muttered Chapman in a disgruntled tone. 'You a marshal or a Texas Ranger?' There was a note of suspicion in his tone.

'Not exactly. Let's just say that this hombre owes me somethin'. A debt that has to be paid – in full.'

Chapman narrowed his eyes. He recognised at once that he was dealing with a mighty dangerous and mean character. Yet he wanted no trouble in town. Clem Tollison had been emphatic on that point. For a moment he wondered if this was some Wes Hardin or Billy the Kid, riding hell for leather, running to the end of some feud that would come to a brief and bloody finish on the streets of Big Stone Gap. The thought did not give him any comfort. He let his gaze drop to the gun the other wore noticing the smooth black butt, the well-polished leather of the holster. Yes, indeed, he reflected, a truly dangerous man.

'Might I ask the name of this man you're looking for, mister?'

Frenchy shrugged. 'Sure. His name's Dave Kelsey. I've been trailin' him all the way from Clayton.'

'That right?' said Chapman dryly. The deputy near the wall had turned sharply, was eyeing Frenchy with a sharp-bright stare.

As if he had not noticed this, LaVere went on smoothly: 'There's no cause for you to worry about this, Sheriff. I'll take care of it without any trouble. Just tell me if he's here, where I can find him, and once my business is finished, I'll be riding out of here.'

'Well now.' Chapman got to his feet. He felt a little more sure of himself. 'You're quite right, Kelsey does live here. He rode in some time ago, started to rebuild the place his folks had before the war, some ten miles or so out of town. There was big trouble with the Kelseys about a year ago. Some feud with the Tollisons. It finished with the Tollisons wipin' out the Kelsey family and razing the ranch to the ground. Dave rode back to find out what had happened and swore to repay them in blood.'

French waved a negligent hand. 'I'm not interested in this,' he said thinly. 'This business of mine is just between

Kelsey and me. Whatever call the Tollisons have on him makes no difference.'

Chapman shrugged. 'I'm afraid that may not be so,' he said slowly. 'There's a little more to it than that.'

LaVere's face hardened. 'What's that supposed to mean?'

Chapman's smile was sardonic. 'I'm just thinkin' that perhaps the Tollisons have beaten you to it. Kelsey shot and killed Merl Tollison a couple of nights ago. Claimed it was in self-defence. But it was out at his own place and the only other witness, a gunhand named Fenton, was also killed. I had to bring Kelsey in and lock him up, to wait trial for murder.'

Frenchy's eyes brightened ferally. 'Then you've got him here, in the jail.'

'No. Some time durin' the night a bunch of masked men broke him out of jail. That's how my deputy got the bump on the head.' He nodded towards the man at the rifle rack. 'We're reasonably sure that none of these men were the Tollisons. My guess is that they were men from town.'

'Why would they do that?' With an effort Frenchy forced his angry frustration down. This was possibly only a temporary setback to his plans. He needed, however, to get every bit of information he could out of this man.

Chapman shrugged. 'There are plenty of gents in town who were friendly with the Kelseys. They dared not do anythin' openly to help Dave because of their fear of runnin' foul of the Tollisons. But they might break him out of jail if they figured they could do it without being recognised.'

Speaking through tightly clenched teeth, Frenchy asked: 'You figure he'll make a run for it now he's free?'

'Knowing Dave Kelsey, I'd say it ain't likely.' The deputy spoke up, moving forward. 'He said he'd even the score with the Tollisons – and he'll do it, even if he gets himself killed in the process.'

'So he could still be around.' LaVere nodded to himself as if satisfied with the answer. 'Guess I'll have to stick around for a while.

'So long as you don't start any trouble, that's all right with me, I guess.'

Frenchy gave a brief nod. His eyes were like slivers of ice. 'I figured it might be, Sheriff,' he said enigmatically.

Outside, he paused to glance up and down the street, then led his mount along to the livery stable, saw that it was given the best stall in the place then moved over to the saloon.

The others were at the bar when he entered. Mureau drained his glass, looked round as Frenchy came up to him.

'Find out anything?' he asked in a low tone.

'Some,' Frenchy signalled to the bartender, poured himself a drink and downed it in a single gulp. He took more time over his second. 'He's around here some place. Seems he's ridden into the middle of some feud. They had him locked in the jail but some *hombres* busted him out during the night.

'So what do we do now?'

'We stay here and wait. Sooner or later we'll raise the scent. Then this thing will be finished, one way or the other.

6

Sunblast

Slowly Dave Kelsey regained consciousness, wakening to the pounding pain in his skull. After a while, as he lay there, he became aware of the pain in his left ankle, of the vicious pull on it whenever he tried to move his leg. Blinking against the fierce, biting glare of the sun, he struggled up into a sitting position, forcing down the rising sensation of nausea in the pit of his stomach. The chain was securely padlocked to his leg, and through a red-blurred vision he saw that the chain had been fastened to the stake nine feet or so away.

Screwing up his eyes, he tried to think things out clearly, but his brain seemed woolly and thoughts moved sluggishly in his mind as though long passages long unused. How long had he been unconscious? Turning his head with a wrenching of neck muscles, he saw that he was alone. The Tollisons had pulled out, leaving him to his fate. All around him there was only the burning desert, the shimmering horizons and the dust devils whirling and eddying across the sand.

For a moment he remained absolutely still, striving to clear his mind. Then he leaned forward, grasping the chain, pulling it towards him. One glance was sufficient to show him that it had been fastened too securely to his leg for him ever to hope to get it off. The padlock was of stout metal, looped through the broad hasp. The chain itself was of tough steel; nothing short of a hammer and chisel would break those links.

He gave up and lay back as a fresh wave of sickness swept over him, leaving him weak and trembling in every limb. What a goddamn foolish way to die and so far he had only killed one of the Tollisons.

The burning touch of the sun on his naked back and shoulders only served to increase the nagging pain of the deep lacerations. He recognised that he was in pretty poor shape, both physically and mentally, and that his condition was likely to deteriorate rather than improve as the day wore on. Already the heat was rising to its piled-up intensity and, as far as he was able to judge, it was around noon. Not until evening would there be any coolness and, when night came, the temperature could drop well below freezing point, making things even worse. If he was to do anything at all to help himself, he had better start now, rather than waiting.

Thrusting himself to his feet, swaying as the blood rushed pounding to his head, he edged forward towards the stake, then paused. Through his wavering vision, he saw something that gave him fresh hope. The shovel! Somehow the Tollisons, confident in their belief that they had now finished him, had left it behind when they had pulled out. It lay on the edge of a small hollow, ten feet or so from him. Crawling forward, he calculated the distance to it, realised that it was almost beyond his reach. Gritting his teeth as the pain jarred through his ankle, he stretched himself out full length on the burning alkali, straining at the very limit of the chain, fingertips brushing the blade of the shovel.

Scarcely daring to breathe, he tried to grip the smooth metal, blinking his eyes as the sharp flashes of sunlight, striking off it into his eyes, threatened to blind him, sending spasms of agony lancing through his forehead.

Desperately he clawed his way forward, struggling to gain an extra inch. It was impossible to do more than just touch it with his fingers. His arms and legs felt numb. The blistering heat on his body threatened to overwhelm him completely.

Several times he had to pause to force his taut, knotted limbs to relax. Then he tried again, squirming lengthwise over the dust. For a moment his fingers caught at the blade. He felt a sudden surge of exhilaration go through him. With the spade, he had a good chance of digging up that stake. He would still not be completely free, but it would mean that he would be able to move from there, even hampered by the ponderous weight of the chain dragging behind him.

Then the exhilaration vanished abruptly in a single second of despair. He felt the spade move under fingers. It tilted forward, began to slide. Madly he fumbled with it, cursed savagely under his breath as it slid away and fell with a faint clatter into the depression, striking the rocks of the way down to the bottom. He felt like crying aloud with the anguish of that moment. Now the spade might have been on the rocky surface of the moon rather than a few feet away for all the good it would do him.

He must have lost consciousness again then. When he came to his entire body ached. Perspiration covered him from head to foot and the dull, throbbing pain in his head was like a hammer banging away without cease, crashing against the grey walls of his brain. His tongue seemed swollen to twice its normal size, moving sluggishly against his teeth, and his throat was so parched and dry that whenever he attempted to swallow he choked and gagged with the effort.

Stirring himself, he dragged his body across the sand to the stake. He spent several frustrating, weakening minutes, hands clasped around the stout piece of wood, heaving and twisting as he tried to pull it free of the ground. As he worked he lost all sense of time and the stifling, sunburned heat of the day became an unending eternity of pain and fatigue. When he finally became exhausted, he lay back on the sand, face down on his belly to shield his eyes from the vicious glare of the sun which hung like a disc of fire in the blazing, cloudless heavens. He was conscious that there was nothing he could do, that he was wasting his time and energy, but something deep within him forced him to go on, even beyond the usual limit of physical endurance.

There were long moments when it was only his deep, blazing hatred of the Tollisons, and not self-preservation, that kept him working on that stake. There were moments when he even forgot who he was, what he was doing there, his mind empty of everything but the terrible pain which suffused throughout the whole of his body, the only thing he could not entirely close his mind to.

Overhead the sun commenced its slow glide down the western slopes of the sky. The heat, however, continued to climb. Finally the utter weakness in his body overcame everything else. His head sank forward on to the white dust.

Ben Chapman rode through the wide gate leading up to the Tollison ranch with a faint sense of foreboding in his mind. It was late afternoon and the illusion of coolness carried by the freshening breeze was gone as he moved into the shelter of the hills which crowded in on the place to the south-west. Off the point of a ridge which abutted out from the hills, reaching down towards the trail, where a small clump of trees grew out of the thin topsoil, stood a small wooden shack. As he drew level with it, a man stepped out, a rifle in the crook of his arm. He eyed the other suspiciously for a moment, then lowered the gun to his side as he recognised the sheriff.

'You're a little off your usual trail, ain't you Sheriff?' said the other. There was only a thinly disguised deference in the other's tone.

Chapman let it pass. He was well aware how the men on Tollison's payroll regarded him. They had little time for men who played at being lawmen, men who only held down their job because of the whim of some big man such as Clem Tollison.

'I want to see Mister Tollison,' he said tautly. He mopped his streaming brow with his bandanna. 'It's important. Somethin' happened in town today I reckon he'd better know about.'

The other grinned. 'Could be he probably knows about it already,' he answered, 'if you're talkin' about Dave Kelsey being taken from your jail.'

Chapman shook his head. 'It ain't that. It's somethin' else.' He felt a faint perverse sense of satisfaction as he noticed the sudden change in the other's expression. 'Now do I get to see him – or not?'

'Guess it'll be all right,' said the guard after a moment's consideration. 'They rode back here half an hour ago. You'll find 'em up at the ranch house.'

'Thanks,' said Chapman tonelessly. He gigged his mount, following the trail until it led over the brow of a low hill, down into the wide courtyard. He noticed that there were more than a couple of dozen horses in the corral and several men lounging nonchalantly in front of the bunkhouse.

As he reined up, the porch door opened and Creede Tollison came out, eyed him speculatively for a moment, then said: 'Not too often we see you ridin' this way, Chapman. What's on your mind? Come to tell us that Kelsey got away from jail?' His tone and the look in his eyes was mocking.

'Not exactly. Got somethin' else on my mind I figure your Pa ought to know about.'

Creede took a cigar from his coat pocket, thrust it between his lips with a faintly aggressive movement and lit it, puffing smoke in front of him for several moments before speaking. Then he said: 'Guess you'd better light down then and come inside to speak your piece.'

Ben Chapman dismounted, followed the other into the house. He found Clem Tollison seated behind a polished oak desk in one of the large airy rooms. The windows were open, letting in a little of the air.

'Sheriff Chapman wants a word with you, Father,' Creede said, ushering him inside. 'Says it's important.'

Clem Tollison looked up. His face was without expression. He paused for a moment, then waved a hand towards the chair in front of the desk. 'Sit down, Ben,' he said quietly. 'What's on your mind?'

'I thought I'd better take a ride out and warn you that some men rode into town a couple of hours ago. One of 'em, a fellow by the name of Frenchy LaVere, came into the office asking about Dave Kelsey.'

Tollison's interested quickened, but his laugh was short and cynical. 'Did he give any reason why he wanted him?'

'Only that it was some kind of business between Kelsey and himself. I had him figured for a marshal at first. Now I'm pretty sure he's some killer, gunnin' for Kelsey.'

'And just what did you tell him, Chapman?' demanded Creede from the doorway.

'Only that he'd been busted out of jail last night and taken out of town. I said I figured some of the townsfolk must have done it, hoping to get him away before his neck was stretched..'

Creede relaxed visibly. He flashed a quick grin. 'Let's hope he's satisfied with that. We don't want anybody else hangin' around town. Could complicate things for us.'

'Where is this hombre now, Ben?' asked Tollison gently. He offered the other a cigar, lit it for him.

'He said he'd stick around for a while, just to see if Kelsey turned up.'

'Guess there's no harm in that.' The other sat back in his chair, stared contemplatively out of the window for a moment. 'Keep an eye on him, Ben. Let me know every move he makes while he's in town. Everything. You understand?'

'Sure, Mister Tollison, I'll do that.' Chapman got to his feet, stood for a moment looking down at the rancher. 'Do you figure there's any chance of Kelsey riding back into town?'

'I doubt it,' said Tollison. 'Somehow, I doubt that very much.' He leaned his head back, eyes half closed, as the other left the room. He was still sitting there listening to the sound of the sheriff's horse moving out of the court-yard and heading up into the hills. Slowly the muffled abrasion died away into the distance and, a moment later, the door opened and Creede came in.

There was silence for a little while, the other walking over to the window, his face creased into worried lines.

'You concerned by what Chapman told us?' The older man asked presently.

'Some,' agreed the other. 'I don't like the way something has been added to this business. Something over which we have no control.'

The other shrugged, flicked the length of grey ash from his cigar with an exaggerated gesture. 'You got a reason?'

'Just call it a feeling between the shoulder blades,' Creede replied. 'And the trouble is, I've always found in the past that this feeling means somethin'.'

'Forget it.' Clem pushed back his chair, got to his feet and moved over beside the other. 'Kelsey is either dead by now or pretty close to it, and whoever this *hombre* is, we've nothin' to fear from him. If he came gunning for Kelsey, it's just too bad. We've done it for him. Maybe he should be real grateful to us for savin' him the trouble.'

Speaking, he turned his head a little so that the slanting rays of the mid-afternoon sun fell upon his craggy features. His eyes narrowed down a little. 'If it'll make you feel better, we'll ride out tomorrow mornin' just to be sure Kelsey is dead. If this killer who rode into town wants to start somethin', then we'll finish it for him.'

*

For the best part of three hours the small clearing dotted about by scrub and stunted brush lay still and hot under the fierce, unrelenting drive of the sun. Only the long length of heavy chain glittered brilliantly in the stark brilliance, throwing flashes of light through the long, sun-hazed afternoon. Then there came movement; slow and hesitant. Dave Kelsey stirred ponderously on the heated ground, lifting his head from the dust, striving to spit it out of his clogged mouth. It had worked its way into his eyes and nostrils, formed a thick cake on his face, blending with the streams of perspiration, itching and irritating. Through the sodden, sluggish thickness of his thoughts, he recalled slowly where he was, the full extent of his predicament. Flopping his left arm across his face to shield his eyes against the sunglare, he rolled over on to his side, forced to concentrate all of his attention and energy on each separate movement he made. With a sudden gust of effort, he succeeded in getting to his knees, where he hung, head down, body swaying slightly like a drunken man. Every muscle and fibre seemed to have worked itself loose within him so that it refused to obey his flagging will. He felt himself tilting to one side, jerked himself upright, drawing air along his raw throat and down into his tortured, aching lungs.

Working his way over to the stake, he rested while his cramped muscles uncoiled and a little life flowed back into them. The outlines of the stake wavered and blurred in front of him and there was a blue-green haze dancing tantalisingly in front of his eyes. Braced on his left elbow, he grasped the upright piece of wood, curling his fingers desperately about it, struggling to rock it to and fro in the sand.

For a pain-filled eternity nothing happened. Then, slowly, gradually, the stake began to move, only by a minute fraction at first, but there was no doubt that it was moving. He could see the tiny grains of sand drifting around the base of it, forming and re-forming intricate patterns under his gaze. For a long while after that nothing in the world seemed to exist but those countless tiny grains of sand that shifted each time he threw his strength on the stake.

When he became exhausted, he fell back and lay unmoving until a little strength returned to his badly punished body. Over his head, wheeling in their silent circles, gliding endlessly, the buzzards hovered over the scene, scenting by some strange instinct the presence of death below them, but not willing to move in until all movement ceased.

By the time the light began to fade the stake was beginning to move appreciably. But the intervals between his efforts were becoming longer and more frequent. He recognised that his strength was almost spent; and more and more it was becoming increasingly obvious to him that even if he did succeed in pulling the stake free of the ground, he would lack the necessary strength to get away from there. If he did not manage to get out of the desert by dawn, his chances of survival out there during another day were almost non-existent.

With nightfall, the numbing cold brought a fresh danger. His hands lost all feeling and he could no longer work by touch. Throwing all of his weight on the stake, he heaved and pulled, his forehead throbbing continually now, giving him no let-up from the pain. The hours passed slowly, things drawn from sheer nightmare. By the time the moon came up, flooding the place with a cold, white radiance, he was on his feet, straining and heaving upwards, both hands twined around the wood, ignoring the blood, the cuts and scratches.

Bracing his legs, he thrust upward with all of the strength left in him, still not expecting to budge the stake, and it was for this reason that when it came out of the ground with a sudden surge, he was totally unprepared for

it and lost his balance, sprawling on to his back in the
sand. He hit hard, lay still for a moment, all of the air
knocked out of his lungs.

Slowly he dragged himself to his feet. For a moment he
knew a fevered urgency. He had no idea how much of the
night still remained. Overhead the stars were bright and
clear, the moon hanging low against the hummocky horizon. Scrambling up, he moved away, heading north-east.
The chain about his leg went suddenly taut, jerking him
off his feet. Cursing, he moved back, picked up the heavy
stake, knowing he would have to carry it too. Then a
thought struck him. Making his way to the shallow depression, he located the shovel lying at the bottom. He ran a
thumb along the edge. Although not as sharp as he would
have wished, he felt certain it would prove suitable to
smash through the wood. Finding a flat rock, he laid the
stake on it, raised the shovel high over his head and
brought the edge of the blade slicing down. It bit deep
into the wood and he struck again and again, somehow
finding a hidden reserve of strength deep within him now
that freedom was so close. Splinters flew in all directions
as he battered frenziedly at the stake until it parted.
Bending, he wrenched the two pieces apart, slid the chain
off and gathered it up, holding it clumsily as he staggered
off into the moonlit darkness. At first he attempted to
run, but there were too many potholes in the ground
which he could not see clearly, deep holes that were big
enough for a man to get his foot into without warning,
snapping his ankle like a match. He proceeded more
cautiously.

When the first greying streaks of the dawn showed in
the east, he had travelled about two miles, and already the
terrible strain was beginning to tell on him. He fell continually now, picking himself up and staggering on. At times
he scarcely knew what he was doing, nor where he was
headed. The world and everything in it dissolved into a
haze of pain and weariness. All about him the tricky moon-

thrown shadows were his only companions. Nothing else moved in a cold and eerie world.

In the grey half-light he stumbled on the small water-hole by accident. He had not expected to find water here. There were still several miles of desert to cross before he reached the low foothills. But topping a low rise, he saw the glint of light off water, saw the small pool of water at the bottom of the gravelly slope, and in his hurry to get to it, tripped over the entangling length of the chain and went sprawling full length down the slope, rolling over several times.

Crawling forward on his elbows, he edged towards the pool, scooped up water in the palm of his hand, sniffed it, then drank. It tasted slimy and icily cold, stale. But it was water and, after he had drunk his fill, he painfully washed the coating of dust from his face and neck, then lay there, letting some of the life and strength soak back into his bruised and battered body. The cool wetness soothed the ache and pain in his head and face. Gradually he felt better. Around him the grey light lengthened and then the sun came up, flooding the desert with a deep red glow that rapidly changed to glaring yellow. He crawled over to a small clump of bushes which grew a few feet from the water's edge, stretched himself out in their shade and closed his eyes.

For a while he found his thoughts straying to Stacy Herbison. Strange how a girl could have changed so much in only four short years, he mused drowsily. Yet, if he looked at things objectively, he had changed far more than she had and in many more ways. The war had bred a ruthlessness in him, a toughness of fibre which he had not previously thought existed. During the long months of fighting in the wilderness, he had looked forward to the time when he might return home, to a sheltered and relatively easy life. Now that was no longer possible. There were forces at work here which were just as ruthless as he was, possibly more so.

Just before his weary brain fell asleep, the picture of Stacy as he had last seen her in the small restaurant in Big Stone Gap drifted before his eyes. She seemed to be smiling at him, telling him that everything would turn out all right in the end if only he had the courage, the necessary strength of will to see it through.

Crossing the final stretch of eroded yellow gullies and clusters of cat-claw to the clearing, the three riders swung down from their saddles, stood looking about them in the bright sunglare. Clem Tollison moved forward, then stiffened into immobility. With slow care he turned, and when he spoke there was a brittle anger in his tone.

'He got away.'

'He couldn't have,' muttered Creede thinly. He moved around in a wide circle, searching the ground. 'You sure this is the right place?'

'Damned sure.' The elder man bent, picked up the splintered pieces of wood, turned them over in his hand for a moment without speaking, his features tight with a full understanding of what must have happened. 'He got hold of that goddamn shovel and smashed through the stake.'

'You've only got yourselves to blame.' Jeb spoke up from the edge of the clearing. 'I wanted to kill him there and then, but you were both so sure he couldn't escape. You wanted him to die a lingerin' death. I just wanted to be sure he died. Now it seems he's out on the loose somewhere and we'll never find him until it's too late.'

Clem swung on his son with a swift, almost menacing movement. 'Shut up,' he ordered thinly. 'I still give the orders around here.' He lifted his head, shaded his eyes with his hand and stared off into the sun-hazed distances. 'He can't have got far, that's certain. Not draggin' that chain along with him. It must weigh close on fifty pounds if not more and, in his condition, things will be even more difficult.' He moved around slowly, keeping his keen-eyed gaze on the ground. The fact that there was no sign of the length of chain gave him renewed hope that it would not prove difficult to locate Kelsey.

Creede straightened up from his examination of the shallow hole in the sand. He rubbed his chin thoughtfully. 'He could be a lot closer than we think,' he said slowly, deliberately. His eyes showed a deep brightness. 'Take a look at this.'

'What is it?' Clem asked, bending beside him.

Creede pointed. 'These marks here. He must've wriggled around here at full length. My guess is he tried to reach the shovel but didn't quite make it. You can see where it slipped down into this depression. Then there's the hole. He could only have worked that stake loose. I'd say he had to pull it out of the ground before he hacked himself free of it.'

'So what difference does it make how he did it?' muttered Jeb bitterly.

Clem silenced him with a sharp gesture of his right hand. 'I see what Creede is gettin' at. If he had to do it that way, it would have taken him the best part of yesterday to work that stake out of the ground. That means he can only have been free for a few hours at most. How far could a man in his condition, draggin' that chain, travel in that time?'

Jeb nodded as slow understanding came to him. 'Not more'n a mile or so,' he agreed. 'Once we find out which way he went we can catch up with him in half an hour.'

Clem heaved himself to his feet. 'Too many tracks around here. We made plenty ourselves yesterday, and gettin' here this mornin'. We split up, go in three directions. In this country it shouldn't be too difficult to spot him half a mile off.'

'Then what are we waitin' for?' Jeb moved towards his horse. 'I'll head north. It's the most likely way he'd go. That way' – he gestured towards the shimmering desert to the south – 'leads nowhere for close on fifty miles. No man in his right senses would start walkin' in that direction, hampered like he is.'

'You could be right,' nodded Clem. 'On the other hand, after a day in the broilin' sun he might not be in his right mind. Another point is that he'll know that if we do return, we'll almost certainly start lookin' for him to the north. So he could try to be too clever for us and deliberately move south until he's sure he's not bein' followed.'

'We're just wastin' time arguin' about which way he may have gone,' broke in Creede. 'Let's get after him. An unarmed man stranded somewhere in the desert ought to pose no problems to us.' He swung up into the saddle, eased the long-barrelled Winchester from its scabbard and checked it before thrusting it back.

Dave Kelsey woke to the harsh glare of sunlight shining in his eyes. With an effort he pushed himself up on to his arms. He must have been asleep for two hours or more, he decided, judging by the position of the sun. It was time to be moving on. Ahead of him the low foothills that lay humped on the horizon shivered in the heat as if he were viewing them through a layer of water. He swallowed thickly, drank his fill of the brackish water in the pool, then got upright, stumbled down the slope, up the far side, feet slipping in the shifting sand, and came into the mesquite and Spanish Sword. Now he no longer tried to carry the hampering weight of the chain, but dragged it over the sand behind him. It made walking difficult, but eased the ache in his back and shoulder muscles. Slowly, haltingly, deathly weary and barely able to stay erect, he lurched into the narrow gullies that opened up without warning in front of him, eyes fixed on the ground a few yards in front of his shaking feet.

He was virtually naked to the waist, arms and shoulders, back and chest laced with deep welts and cuts, flesh streaked with blood and dirt. Blood still seeped slowly from a long gash along his left arm, and his ankle had been rubbed raw almost to the bone by the cruel bite of the metal fastened tightly around it. His chest and lungs hurt intolerably each time he sucked a gust of air down, and his eyes were bloodshot from the effort of staring fixedly into the refracted glare off the desert.

When he could spare the breath for it, he cursed the Tollisons and all they stood for. Even though he was free, it was becoming increasingly obvious that his chances of survival were little better than they had been when he had been chained to that stake. The upthrusting thorny growths of the Spanish Sword made it impossible to walk in a straight line. He had continually to circle around them swaying drunkenly from side to side, trying to study his direction, knowing how easy it was, in country such as this, to walk blindly in a circle until he dropped from sheer exhaustion.

Only his savage anger at the Tollisons, and the occasional thoughts of Stacy Herbison, all blending together into a kind of delirium in his fevered brain, helped him to shut out the agonising pain from his mind and conquer the utter weariness in his body. He longed just to lie down on the hot, burning alkali and surrender himself to the fatigue in his limbs, and the dread knowledge that once he did it would mean the end for him made it all the more desirable. No more need to keep moving, to continue the tremendously punishing effort of putting one foot in front of the other in this endless rhythm of pain, haunted by the clanking rattle of the chain as it struck the outcrops of rock behind him, dogging his heels like some personal devil which never left him.

He breasted a steep rise, took a couple of steps forward, then stopped abruptly, recoiling instinctively. He stood on the edge of a deep gully. A few inches from him the rocky ledge fell sheer for ten feet or so to a stony bottom. He stared out of his blurred vision, paused, then went down on to his knees. At least the floor of the gully was free of brush and other impeding growths, and it seemed to stretch straight ahead for almost half a mile. It was not deep enough to provide shade from the high sun, but with the chain on his ankle continually snagging in the brush, it would make progress easier for him.

On the point of slithering down into it, he paused to throw a quick glance over his shoulder, an instinctive movement, not that he expected to see anything. But there was something there, something which caught his attention and held it. Screened by the thick foliage, he peered out across the level stretch of ground. The dust cloud seemed little bigger than a man's hand held up against the tremendous backdrop of the desert. But it signified danger, meant that there was a rider out there, spurring his mount in his direction.

Very few travellers used the desert if they could possibly help it. The sun-bleached bones of those who had tried and failed bore mute testimony to the dangers which were all too prevalent. Blinking the dust from his eyes, he watched and waited, every muscle in his body poised and tensed. After a while he became certain that there was only one rider there. Either the other was an innocent traveller using the desert trail as a quick, short, but dangerous way of getting to Big Stone Gap from the south, or it was one of the Tollisons.

It came to him then that they might have returned to the scene to assure themselves that he was indeed dead. Clem Tollison was not the sort of man to take unnecessary chances, especially with so much at stake. When they discovered he was gone, they would realise the utmost urgency of finding him before he could get back to town and make further trouble for them. If they were unsure of the direction he had taken, they would split up, search the whole of the surrounding areas.

Very slowly he lowered himself over the lip of the gully, clawing with his hands on the smooth wall as he fell to the rocky bottom, bracing his legs when he hit, then letting himself relax. Had the other spotted him? he wondered tensely. If he had, then what chance did he have against an armed man? All that the other would have to do would be to stand off some distance away and pick him off with a rifle.

Lifting his head, he looked at the rim line above him, then moved cautiously along the gully until he reached the point where the steep walls began to slope down and he was able to peer over the top while remaining hidden behind the thin fringe of scrub. The rider came closer, but for a long while the cloud of dust lifted by the horse's hooves hid the man from view.

Then, when the other was less than a quarter of a mile away, the dust cleared sufficiently for Dave to be able to recognise the man. It was Jeb Tollison.

He drew his lips back across his teeth. It did not seem that the other had spotted him for he was moving on a track that would carry him well clear of the gully. Then, without warning, the other slowed his mount. Dave cursed inwardly as he realised what had happened. Jeb had spotted his trail in the sand. Reining up, Tollison sat for a moment, undecided, then eased the Winchester from its scabbard, wheeling his mount towards the gully.

7

Kelsey Hits Out

Dave felt a chill settle on him. The other was suspicious, but not certain of his presence there. Gently he lowered himself to his knees, looking about him for some kind of weapon. His fingers fastened around a rock, held it for a moment, then he put it down again. Although it was better than nothing, it came to him suddenly that he possessed a much better weapon against Jeb Tollison. The ten-foot length of chain attached to his leg. He fumbled with it, holding it like a lariat. Everything would depend on speed, accuracy and split-second timing.

Tollison moved his horse closer to the lip of the gully, the rifle held in his right hand, his finger on the trigger. As it came closer, the other's mount seemed to sense his presence there for it began bucking and shying away a little. Dave heard Tollison curse savagely under his breath, saw him through the scrub kick his spurs into the animal's flanks, urging it on. The man's eyes ranged all about him. Then he began to move the horse off to the right of where Dave lay. Evidently he had seen the tracks leading along to the edge of the gully.

Time paced slowly to an eternity. Tensing himself, gripping the chain tightly in his right hand, his legs braced under him, he waited until the other was less than ten feet away, then whirled the chain once around his head, using all of his strength in the attempt, letting it go as the other swung his head instinctively at the sudden movement.

Desperately Tollison tried to level the Winchester on him, to depress it sufficiently to bring it to bear. The end of the chain missed his head by scant inches as he jerked himself back in the saddle with a low cry, but the chain, looping down as its impetus was spent, got tangled in the horse's legs as it reared with a shrill whinny of fright and made to lunge forward. What happened next was almost too swift to be taken in. The horse surged forward for a couple of yards, the chain tautening as it dragged away from the gully. Then it crashed headlong as its forelegs tangled with it, bringing it down. With a wild cry, Jeb Tollison shot out of the saddle, fell heavily on the sand, the rifle spinning from his hand.

In that moment Dave had his first flash of clear, coherent thought since sighting the other. He had started something here that it was going to take a great deal of doing, shackled to the chain as he was, but it was a chance he might never get again. Sheer wild rage would not be good enough, even though this was the emotion that threatened to overwhelm him in that instant. Here he would need speed and cunning and quick thinking, as well as all of his remaining resources of strength and endurance.

Hauling himself over the rim of the gully, he stumbled towards the fallen figure of Jeb Tollison as the other tried to push himself up on to his knees. Somehow the horse had managed to struggle up, stamping itself free of the impeding chain. But Dave noticed this only with a part of his attention.

Savagely he threw his weight at Tollison, striking the other on the shoulder, hurling him back on to the ground once more. They struck, rolling and heavy, but the impact drove them apart. Gasping, Jeb Tollison tried to reach for the Colt at his waist. His fingers had only half cleared it of leather when Dave hit him hard on the wrist with the chain. Yelling harshly with agony, Tollison dropped the gun, clawed up with his free hand for Dave's throat, the steel-like fingers closing on his windpipe, squeezing inexorably, with all of the strength the other could muster.

Bracing himself, feeling his strength slipping away as he struggled to draw air down into his lungs, Dave kicked hard at the other's shins, grabbed for his wrists and tried to force them down. Tollison's grip slackened and Dave did not wait for him to recover, but swung two hard, chopping blows to the other's head, taking one himself on his shoulder. Bleeding, half stunned, by the heavy fall, Jeb came surging up, his superb vitality and strength were forces too great to be denied by a man in Dave's condition. He felt himself being forced backward as Tollison threw him aside, grinning fiercely through bloodied lips.

'I figured I'd find you here, Kelsey,' grunted the other in harsh gasps. 'That's why I chose to head in this direction. But I didn't reckon on you gettin' so far. Now I'm goin' to kill you with my bare hands.'

'That's what you think.' Dave lunged forward, a bunched fist driving ahead of him.

Tollison saw it coming, twisted his head to one side, riding it on his shoulder. Even so, Dave's fist skidded on and took him partly on the neck, knocking him sideways, temporarily off-balance. Dave fell in against the other, sagging against him, felt Tollison's arms go around his middle in a bear hug. The grip tightened as the other got his head down against Dave's breastbone, out of the way of his fists, fingers interlocked in the small of his back.

Straining desperately, Dave held on to the other, pulling him, close, trying to remain straight and on his feet, knowing that once Tollison got him on the ground in this grip, it would all be over. He felt the other lift his knee, twisted instinctively as it came driving for his groin, taking the blow on his thigh instead. The sudden move took Tollison by surprise. His foot slipped in the treacherous sand. Falling sideways with a startled oath, he teetered on one leg for an instant, striving to maintain his balance. Dave seized his opportunity, kicked at the other's leg, hitting it hard with the toe of his boot. Tollison stumbled, went down, with Dave on top of him. The grip of Jeb's arms loosened. With an effort, Dave sucked air down into his lungs. He seemed to be seeing the other through a wavering red haze that obscured details, so he saw only a vague grey blue where Tollison's face was supposed to be. The long, arduous efforts of the past twenty-four hours were now taking their toll of him. He knew he could not keep this up much longer. He had to end it as soon as possible – and permanently.

Kicking out with his left foot, he felt it sink into the soft flesh of the other's middle, driving him back, and there was a breaking agony in his wild cry. He doubled forward, clutching at his belly with both hands, fingers interlocked, a greyness in his face now, lips working soundlessly. But in spite of the fact that the advantage was his, Dave found it impossible to move. There was a weakness and a burning agony in his body which held him immobile on the ground as Tollison stood swaying over him. Indeed, it was the other who managed to recover first. Drawing in a great gust of air, Tollison looked about him for some weapon, then bent swiftly, grabbing at the end of the chain. There was a fiendish grin on his battered features as he swung it around his head in a glittering circle.

Through wide, staring eyes, Dave watched as the other made ready to smash his brains out with the length of steel. Clawing at the sand beside him, he tried to drag himself out of the way, but the other advanced slowly on him, knowing he had all the time in the world, that he had his man at his mercy.

Scrabbling in the sand, Dave's fingers encountered something hard and metallic. For a moment he thought it was simply the chain, then he recognised it for what it was. Tollison's Colt that had fallen from his fingers during the fight. Even as the end of the chain came whistling for his head, he jerked up the gun, finger tightening on the trigger, barely taking aim as he fired.

The gun jerked hard against his wrist. The slug took Tollison high in the chest. Through his blurring vision, Dave saw the other halt in his track, sway back, a look of stunned, incredulous surprise on his face. The drifting cloud of gunsmoke dissipated. There was a red, growing stain on the front of Jeb Tollison's shirt. The chain slipped from between his fingers as though it had suddenly grown too heavy for him to hold, clattered across Dave's legs.

For what seemed an eternity, Tollison remained standing there, swaying drunkenly. Then he went back on his heels, legs buckling under him. Breathing heavily, Dave struggled to a sitting position, stared at the other. The shot had finished it. The fight had been short, sharp and brutal. Now it was over.

Acting on impulse, Dave crawled over to the other, began to search through the man's pockets. It was a far out chance, but it paid off. In Tollison's jacket pocket he found a key. Scarcely daring to believe his good fortune, he tried it in the padlock of the chain. Less than a minute later he was free.

The shadows were beginning to lengthen by the time Dave rode across the narrow plank bridge which led into town. He rode warily, keeping his eyes open for trouble. As yet he had no way of knowing what had been happening in town during the past few days. Circling around, he moved along the back alleys, shunning the main street with the yellow lights beginning to show in the windows.

There was the yellow glow of lamplight showing in the front window of the small restaurant and he picked out the sound of voices from inside. Not wanting to run into any of the other townsfolk until he was more sure of himself, he dismounted, moved around to the rear of the building and knocked softly on the door.

It swung open a few moments later and he saw Stacy framed in the opening. 'Who – Dave!' She gave a faint smile of welcome, then her expressive face showed her surprise and concern at his appearance. 'What happened to you?'

With an effort, Dave managed to dig up a weary smile. The sight of the girl was a heart-warming tonic as far as he was concerned. 'I've been busy with the Tollisons,' he said succinctly. He stumbled on the step as he moved forward and Stacy caught hold of his arm, helping him inside, closing the door softly behind him.

Dave dropped wearily into the chair at the long table in the small kitchen, resting himself on his elbows. Stacy put the coffee pot on to the stove, then came back and sat down opposite him. 'You look as if you tried to take them all on single-handed,' she said softly. 'I'll clean those wounds of yours and then you'll stay here for the night. A good rest will soon put you back on to your feet, and it's a certainty you can't move through the town in that condition.'

Dave knew better than to protest when she used that tone of voice. Weakly, he submitted as she got hot water and lint, bathed and bandaged his back and shoulders. Then she brought him hot coffee, waited until he had drunk it down and eaten a few biscuits before asking him any questions.

'You certainly had us worried,' she said quietly, regarding him closely. 'We heard that you had been taken from the jail, and it wasn't difficult to guess that the Tollisons were behind it.'

'They were,' Dave affirmed grimly. 'They staked me out in the desert for buzzard meat. But they forgot to take away the shovel and I managed to hack my way free.'

'But how did you manage to get back here?'

Dave forced a quick grin. 'They wanted to be sure I'd died. They must have come to check on me this morning at first light. When they discovered I'd gone, they split up to search for me. I bumped into Jeb Tollison on the way back here.' He paused for a moment, then went on harshly. 'He's dead, Stacy. I had to kill him. It was either him or me.'

'And the others?' She looked at him directly as she spoke, her lips laid closely together in a full line.

'I don't know. Maybe they're still out there in the desert, lookin' for me. Or they've given up and ridden back. Soon they're goin' to find out what happened to Jeb. Then there'll be hell to pay in town. That's why I'm not sure I ought to stay here. I can guess the way Clem Tollison will react if he finds out that you've helped me.'

The girl gave an imperious toss of her head. 'I'm not afraid of Tollison. I doubt if my father is. There are also several people in town who're beginning to see the sort of man he really is. They only need a lead to start something. I'm sure of it. If they see that you can fight them and get away with it, they may fall in with you.'

'Somehow, I doubt that. Tollison has ridden roughshod over them for far too long for them to move against him now. Besides, he still has that private army of hired gunslingers out at his place, ready to move in if he gives the word.'

'And what about that friend of yours? Do you think he will come back with help for you?'

Dave shrugged. 'I don't know. This is really no fight of his. He only promised to do so because he felt he owed me somethin'.'

Stacy nodded. Her expression was thoughtful. Sipping her coffee, she said: 'I think you should know there is someone else in town who has been asking around for you.'

Dave brought up his head sharply at that. 'Do you know who it is?'

'A man by the name of LaVere. Small, sharp-featured.'

'I know him.'

'Why does he want you,' Dave?'

'It's a long story. It's the reason Marengo feels he owes me somethin'. We bumped into LaVere in a town called Clayton. He's a cardsharp, a crooked gambler and killer with a string of dead men to his credit. I caught him out cheatin' Marengo. He tried to go for his gun, but I pulled a bluff on him. Then he attempted to kill me with the help of two friends of his. He swore he'd come after me and finish the job. But I didn't expect him to trail me as far as this. It adds a new complication to everythin'.'

'There'll be plenty of time to worry about that in the morning,' said Stacy firmly. 'You're in no condition, physically or mentally, to worry about it now.' She rose to her feet. 'I'll make up a bed for you. We'll talk more about it in the morning.'

'I hope you're right about me bein' safe here,' he said, as she moved to the door. 'Things are goin' to break in this town pretty soon that we may not be able to control.'

'If it has to happen, it will,' murmured the girl. She paused for a moment, then went out and closed the door behind her. When she came back ten minutes later. Thomas Herbison was with her. He looked much older than when Dave had last seen him only a few days before. His forehead was creased with deep lines of worry and concern.

'Howdy, Dave,' he said in greeting. 'Stacy has been tellin' me what happened to you. Seems to me you're gettin' deeper and deeper into trouble all the time.'

'That's the way I see it,' Dave agreed. He felt his eyelids beginning to go together from lack of sleep, forced himself straighter in the chair. 'I've been hearin' about Frenchy LaVere ridin' into town lookin' for me.'

'He seems to be a bad one. Maybe more of a snake than the Tollisons. If he links up with them, you won't have a chance.' Concern and doubt were uppermost in the other's tone as he stood looking down at Dave. Kelsey guessed that he wasn't quite as glad at having him stay there for the night as Stacy was. Certainly he had a lot to lose if the Tollisons should decide to move against him. It had taken him years to build up this small business. It could all be wiped out in a single hour.

Stacy said: 'Can't you see he's dead beat, Dad? If you have to talk to him, it'll wait until tomorrow.' She took up a lamp, moved from the room with it. Dave followed her. She put the lamp down on the small table beside the bed in the back room, turned down the wick so that there was only a faint yellow glow visible. Her face was in shadow as she moved back to the door, pausing beside him. Reaching out, he caught her arm, turned her to face him.

'Stacy,' he said softly. 'I don't know why you're doin' all this for me. In the old days before the war we seemed to be always fightin' each other.'

He saw the faint gleam of her teeth in the shadow of her face as she smiled. 'That was all a long time ago, Dave,' she murmured. 'Those days are past and gone. Things can change in four years.' Even as she finished speaking she stood on tiptoe, pulled her face down to hers. There was a warmth about her, swelling through him, a softness that he had never experienced before.

Then she pulled away from him. 'Goodnight, Dave.' He heard the door close softly in the dimness.

Stretching himself out on the bed, feeling the coolness of the sheets on his bruised, torn flesh, he lay and listened to the night sounds of the town outside the window. His thoughts were a turmoil inside his weary mind. When he had ridden into town, there had been the growing feeling inside him that the end of trouble might be in sight. But now, with the news that Frenchy LaVere was there, all of the cold dread had returned. He knew how dangerous was the ground on which he stood. So many things could happen, events which at the present time he could not hope to foresee. If only he knew how things might pan out, he could take precautions against them. But he was more in the dark now than he had ever been.

He closed his eyes, breathing deeply and evenly. Gradually the sounds outside ceased. Silence hovered over the streets of Big Stone Gap. One by one the yellow lights began to go out. Soon, only those in the saloons were left on as the late-night revellers continued to drink at the bars. These, and a single yellow glow that showed in one of the windows of the hotel on the corner of the square were the only ones to stay on an hour after midnight when the rest of the town lay in darkness.

Frenchy LaVere had taken a room at the hotel, making certain that it was on the upper floor and overlooking the main street. He had remained in that room all through the long, hot afternoon, keeping an eye on the traffic that passed up and down the street, watching for the one face he was looking for, the man he had followed for so many weary miles across an entire state. He had left the room only at supper time, going down into the small dining room, eating his meal alone, before climbing back up the stairs. The rest of his men were scattered around town, but they had their orders and shortly before eleven o'clock that night they all came up to the room.

Frenchy's earlier conviction that Kelsey had been pulled out of the jail by a handful of the town's citizens, determined not to let him hang, was still uppermost in his mind; but he was now becoming a little troubled over his inability to find Kelsey. Mureau had ridden out to the burnt-out ruins of the former Kelsey homestead and had returned shortly after noon with the news that although the other had obviously been there, and recently, there was now no sign of him and the ashes in the hearth were cold. The rest of the men had scouted around town, asking discreet questions, but again having no success. It appeared as if Kelsey had simply vanished off the face of the earth. There was, of course, one other distinct possibility, but he did not want to admit it. Namely, that the

Tollisons, anxious to wreak their own personal vengeance on Kelsey, had been behind the break from jail. If this were so, then it could easily mean that Kelsey was already dead and he had been denied the satisfaction of killing him himself.

Stretching out his legs in front of him, he smoked a cigar and let his gaze wander over each of the men in the room in turn. Finally he fixed his eyes on Mureau. 'He's got to be somewhere around the place, unless they're spirited him away somewhere well away from town. Maybe he's hidin' out up there in the hills.'

Mureau shrugged. 'Goddam,' he said thickly. 'Do you realise how big those hills are? Close on a hundred miles long and fifty wide, with a thousand places a man can hide out, and stay hidden for a year. We'd never have a chance if we tried to comb that place.'

'Then there's got to be another way of goin' about this.' French ran the tip of his finger down the side of his nose. 'Sooner or later he's goin' to make a try for the Tollisons. From what I hear, this feud goes pretty deep. Maybe if we were to keep an eye on them, he'd come to us.'

Mureau compressed his lips into a thin, hard line. 'You reckon that would be wise? It could start a chain of reactions we might not be able to stop. These hombres are plenty mean – and big. They give the orders around here and when they snap their fingers, everybody in town jumps. That is – everybody but Dave Kelsey.'

'And Frenchy LaVere,' snapped the other harshly. 'I jump for no one. Just remember that. I have no fight with the Tollisons. But if they try to get in my way, then they'll regret it.'

One of the other men shook his head. 'I came here to kill Kelsey,' he said solemnly. 'I don't mind helpin' you with a chore like that. But I'm damned if I'll get mixed up with a range war. Too many bullets flyin' from too many directions. A man's more'n likely to end up with a piece of lead in his back.'

'You sayin' you're scared of the Tollisons?' said LaVere, sarcastically.

'Nope. Only that it don't make sense buckin' them when all we came for is one man. I say, get him, finish it, and ride on out of here without lookin' for more trouble.'

'I'm all for that,' muttered one of the other men.

Frenchy drew deeply on his cigar, regarded the redly glowing tip for a long moment, then said in a silky tone: 'That the feelin' of the rest of you?'

One by one the men nodded slowly. 'Clem Tollison has got more than fifty gunslingers at his beck and call,' said Mureau. 'Try to go against him and he'll smash us without even exertin' himself.'

Frenchy got to his feet and took a short turn up and down the room. This was a problem which had already occurred to him and as yet he saw no way around it. In the dull yellow wash of the lamplight there was visible on his face the grey pressure of his turbulent thoughts and the furious anger that was storming up at the back of his eyes.

'Maybe if I was to have a little talk with Tollison, we could come to some kind of agreement. After all, we both want the same thing. I like to do these things the easy way if it's at all possible. Trouble between us would be foolish.'

He went back to his seat, thought the whole proposition over very carefully in his mind as he sat there with his cigar.

When he awoke, Dave found the sunlight streaming in through the bedroom window, laying a pattern of light and shade on the floor near the bed. For a moment he did not remember where he was and lay quite still, staring up at the ceiling, striving to recollect things in his mind, backtracking through the more recent memories. In spite of the sunlight, the room had the faint chill of early morning in it as he swung his legs to the floor, got up and went over to the window. The unaccustomed stiffness in his arms and shoulders soon brought the memories flooding back, and

he winced as pain lanced briefly through his body. The
bitter, savage battle with Jeb Tollison, the long, terrible
trek across the desert. He wet his face from the basin on
the bureau, dried it, then went over to the mirror on the
wall and stared at his reflection in it, noticing the
scratched and purple bruises on his flesh, the puffiness
around his lips. He looked a mess. Small wonder that Stacy
had showed such surprise and concern when she had first
seen him, standing there on the doorstep the previous
night.

But his head was now clear and he felt more alive than
at any time in the past forty-eight hours, ready for
anything that the new day might bring. The feeling of restless exhilaration faded a little as he remembered that
Frenchy LaVere was somewhere in town, bent on a mission
of vengeance. Frenchy was a man it would be extremely
dangerous to underestimate. He belonged in a different
class to Clem Tollison and his sons. They fought with an
ungovernable fury, brought about by the unbridled
passions of the blood feud which had existed for years
between their two families. It was the fury of the mountain
cat.

But Frenchy was a snake, devoid of emotion, full of
cunning, capable of anything to gain his own ends.
Dressing, he went into the kitchen. Stacy was already up,
preparing breakfast. She turned as he entered, flashed
him a warm smile of greeting.

He smiled back at her. It was the first real smile she had
seen from him since he had ridden into town; he seemed
embarrassed, but still cheerful.

'How do you feel now, Dave?' she asked him.

'Hungry. I could eat a whole ox.'

'Well, I can't promise you that,' she said laughing. 'But
I'll see what I can rustle up for you.'

He sat down at the table, watching her as she worked. It
was hard now to remember her as the girl with the hair in
long braids. That memory seemed to belong not only to a

different world, but to a different person.

'When you've eaten, I'll get a razor for you.' She heaped the bacon and beans on to the plate, set them in front of him, then sat down with him, sipping her coffee, but not eating otherwise.

'What can you do now, Dave?' she asked eventually. 'It seems as if everyone is against you.'

He held his silence for several moments and said at last: 'Do you know where Frenchy LaVere is now?'

'He took a room at the hotel on the corner of the square. But there were four men with him when he rode in; maybe more.'

Dave nodded. 'That will be right,' he agreed. 'Frenchy wouldn't take the risk of ridin' in alone.'

'Do you think that Ben Chapman would—'

'Give me the protection of the law?' Dave shook his head bitterly. 'He's in cahoots with Tollison. They've seen to it that I've been branded a killer and an outlaw. Chapman knows he made a mistake arrestin' me and lockin' me in jail the last time. He'll have had his orders to shoot to kill if he gets another chance.'

'So what can you do?'

'Go back to the ranch. There's nothin' else.'

'But won't that be the first place they'll look?'

'Perhaps.' He wiped his plate clean with a piece of bread. 'Or maybe it'll be the last place they'll expect me to go to. But at least I can defend myself there.'

She gave him a long, hard look, then got to her feet, setting down the empty coffee cup. 'I'll get that razor and some hot water for you,' she said gravely.

He took the shaving gear, poured himself the boiling water, and shaved in front of the mirror on the wall of the bedroom. Then he splashed his face with cold water, towelled it quickly. Buckling on the heavy gunbelt which he had taken from Jeb Tollison, he took out the Colt and hefted it in his hand for a moment, feeling the balance of the gun. It had seen plenty of use, he thought, as he thrust

it back into leather; the mechanism worked with a
buttered smoothness, speaking of good care.

Stacy watched him when he came back into the kitchen.
Her glance fell to the gun at his waist, and some of the
softness went out of her features. She recognised his
mood, knew that nothing she might do or say would
dissuade him from what he knew he had to do.

'Take care when you ride out of town, Dave,' she said
softly. 'Even if the Tollisons aren't watching for you,
Frenchy LaVere will have every trail watched.'

'I'll be careful,' he promised. He hitched the gunbelt a
little higher, then moved towards the door. As he reached
it, Stacy came right up to him, kissed him full on the lips,
then stepped back, her eyes deep and dark.

The faint perfume of her hair lingered with him as he
made his way along the narrow alley until he reached the
spot where he had left his mount the previous evening. The
slight pressure of her lips seemed to stay with him as he
mounted up, walked the horse to the end of the alley, out
into another one which led away at right angles from it.

He saw no one but a drunk sleeping off the past night's
indulgences in a corner, legs sprawled out in front of him,
his hat halfway across his eyes. A lean cur sauntered across
the alley just as he approached the edge of town, a
mustard-coloured animal with its ribs showing through
the flesh. It gave him a mournful look, then slunk off into
the long shadows.

Once out of town he gave the horse its head, taking the
twisting trail which led up towards the higher ground.
Half an hour later he crossed a small creek that bubbled
down from the summits of the hills, turned off the trail on
the far side, moving into the tall pines that towered high
above him on either side. He did not intend to move back
on to the trail at all now that he had left it.

The sun was climbing higher into the sky now, but was
still behind the uppermost branches of the tall, stiff pines.
Here, beneath the trees, the air still held some of the chill

of the night, a coldness that would not dissipate fully until
around noon. He rode swiftly, every sense alert for trouble. There was no underbrush here and he made good
progress. The sharply aromatic scent of the pines stayed in
his nostrils all of the way through the forest, and the
faintly green glow of sunlight trapped by the almost solid
mat of leaves and twigs overhead, was restful on the eye.

Once or twice he came across a narrow wagon trail,
easily recognisable where the twin ruts were cut deeply
into the earth. There still seemed to be some traffic
between the valley and the hills, he mused.

By noon he had almost reached the end of the forest,
coming out on a smooth ridge that looked down on to the
valley where it stretched away for several miles to the
north and east. He did not push his mount. Two or three
days ago he had felt a rising urgency to get this chore over
with, but no longer. It had been a form of wild, insane
fury which could not last. If it had, he did not doubt that
he would have been dead by now. With the knowledge
that LaVere was there had come a strange kind of
patience, hardening his anger into a fixed and inflexible
purpose.

He threw off another couple of creeks before he halted,
resting in the shade of a tall redwood that grew out of the
side of the hill like some lonely sentinel. After the first
quick descent from the high ridges, the ground became
more open, cut by deep gullies, broken by short, flat
meadows of tough, wiry grass. He crossed these openly,
anticipating no danger from here, and was passing down
into a wide clearing when his hat was suddenly jerked
from his head, the sharp, flat report of the rifle reaching
him a second later. In an instant he was out of the saddle,
running for cover, bent double to present a more difficult
target to the dry-gulcher. The horse, reins hanging loosely,
remained standing where it was, looking about it inquir-
ingly.

Dropping down behind a grassy mound, Dave lifted his

head cautiously, peering in the direction of a flat ridge of ground from which the shot seemed to have come. He squinted into the flooding sunlight, trying to pick out the faint, drifting cloud of gunsmoke that would give away the other's position, but could make out nothing. The gunman had to be crouched down there somewhere.

Licking his lips, he edged back a little. There seemed to be only one dry-gulcher, otherwise more shots would have been fired at him from other directions before he had had a chance to run for cover.

Grinning a little, he drew his Colt. The man must be waiting for him to show himself again, not daring to expose himself to any return fire. Dave realised that having only a handgun he was at a distant disadvantage. The gunhawk had only to keep at a safe distance and manoeuvre around to enfilade his victim. Somehow, he had to forestall this move. Wriggling back, he reached the end of the ridge, dived forward into a cluster of rocks where he could move forward unseen into a gulch that ran lengthwise across the ridge.

The ground here was in his favour. Sprinting twenty yards or so, he dropped, breathless, into a shallow depression that brought him to a point where he was almost on the same level as the spot where he reckoned the gunman to be hidden. Convinced he was now in the same line as the dry-gulcher, he raised his head cautiously, an inch at a time, peered out into the sunlight. Slowly he let his gaze travel around the grassy slope, scrutinising the brush where the rifleman lurked, but he could distinguish no sign of him. However, he knew the other must still be there, with the open stretch of ground in front of him, watching the spot where Dave had gone down, hoping to catch a second glimpse of him and make sure with his next shot.

One thing he found puzzling now that he looked back on it. Whoever had fired that shot had been no mean marksman. Why had he not killed him while he had had the chance? It was almost as if the shot had been intended as a warning. He digested this thought for a moment, then narrowed his eyes a little as he caught sight of the sudden movement some thirty yards away from where he lay. There was a glint of red from a neckerchief that showed briefly in a Vee between two large moss-covered boulders. Smiling grimly to himself, Dave edged forward, went down on his stomach and slithered several yards on his chest, keeping his head down, making no sound. He entered the narrowness of a defile, slid through it, then paused, elbows raising him just sufficiently to see over the rocks. Mesquite and thorn were bunched all around him, producing ample cover, and a few minutes later he came out on a narrow ledge just behind the man, staring down at the spread-eagled form below him. As yet the man had no inkling of his presence there. The other lay quite still, his mount tethered to a low branch a few yards off to the left. The gunman's cheek was resting against the stock of the rifle as he sighted along it. Presumably he firmly believed that his quarry was still crouched down out of sight behind the distant ridge and that he would not attempt to make a wide and circuitous move around him to come up on his rear.

Raising himself on his haunches, Dave levelled the Colt on the other, his finger bar straight on the trigger. Softly, he said: 'Better let go of that rifle and ease yourself back, friend, or I put a bullet in you.'

He saw the momentary stiffening of the other's shoulders. For a second the man's fingers tightened convulsively on the gun. Then he forced himself to relax, thumbed the safety catch forward and thrust the weapon away from him. He sat up and lifted his hands, turning his head as he did so. Stepping down, Dave moved up to him.

'All right. Now loosen that gunbelt and let it drop. Slowly now. I'm a trifle trigger-happy when it comes to some hombre tryin' to kill me from cover.'

The other shook his head as he slowly unfastened the

heavy buckle, let the gunbelt slip from his fingers on to the rocks. After he had done so, he moved away, seated himself on the ledge and began making himself a smoke, watching Dave as he did so.

'I must say you're a pretty cool customer,' Dave said, alert for every move on the other's part. The man did not look like the ordinary killer-type, but a man could so easily wind up dead if he went by appearances alone. Behind the most genial mask could lurk the mind of a gunslick killer.

Puffing on his cigarette, the other regarded him seriously. Then he grinned. 'You're Dave Kelsey, ain't you, boy?'

'As if you didn't know that already,' said Dave censoriously. 'Just why did you try to kill me back there?'

The man shook his head ponderously. He nodded towards the Winchester lying on the rocks a few feet away. 'Believe me, boy, if I'd meant to kill you that slug would have been in your heart right now.'

'Then why the shot?'

'I had you figured for one of the Tollisons,' answered the other simply. He seemed quite at his ease. Then he grinned. 'Reckon since you came back things have been hottin' up in the territory. Heard you were back at the old ranch, tryin' to fix things up again. Always meant to drop in and have a talk over old times. When I rode over that way day before yesterday, there was nobody around. Didn't quite know what to make of it. Saw tracks of plenty of horses. Thought maybe the Tollison crew had sneaked up on you unawares.'

'Just who are you?' Dave asked, puzzled. 'And why are you out here watchin' the trail for the Tollisons? They friends of yours?'

The other spat in the dust at his feet, twisted his lips into an ugly grimace. 'Friends!' The way he said it convinced Dave that whatever the Tollisons were, they were not friends of this man. 'My name is Cressidy.' He saw the look of recognition on Dave's face, nodded. 'I see you remember.'

'Sure, I remember.' Dave thrust the Colt back into its holster. 'Lew Cressidy. But they told me you'd gone back east.'

Cressidy stared down at the stub of his cigarette. 'That's what everybody figured.' There was a feral gleam in his eyes. 'Most of the others that the Tollisons ran out of the territory went on over the hill and never came back. But I've got me a score to settle with those coyotes and I mean to do it. I've been up here in these hills ever since. Maybe you recall Rusty Frye? Had the homestead next to mine. Tollison dragged him out of his place one night, set him running with the dogs after him. They done near tore him to pieces before Jeb Tollison put a bullet into him. He was the best pard I ever had. Him and me, we were just like brothers. Tollison gave me no chance to pull out, reckoned I'd head east and not bother him again. That was his biggest mistake. I'm still here and now that things are beginnin' to move, I figure my chance is just about here.'

Dave nodded. 'So far, there are only the two of us,' he said grimly. 'We won't be able to do much if Tollison sets his whole crew on to us.'

Cressidy grunted non-committally. 'Don't know about just the two of us, but there's a regular army squattin' in your place right now. Moved in late last night.'

Dave stared at the other in surprise. He felt a sudden stab of apprehension. Had Tollison guessed that he intended to head back to the ranch and forestalled him?

'Tollison's men?' he asked.

'Nope. Didn't recognise any of 'em. Figured they might be friends of yours, watchin' for you. They looked like Mexicans to me.'

'Mexicans!' In his excitement, Dave gripped the other's arm tightly. 'Are you sure?'

'Course I am,' declared the other emphatically. He peered at Dave closely. 'They are friends of yours then.'

'You're darned right they are. With luck, this could mean the end of the Tollisons. Saddle up and let's move out of here.'

Without any further questions, Cressidy got to his feet, tossed away the butt of the cigarette and whistled up his mount, picking up the Winchester and thrusting it into the scabbard. Going down to his own mount, Dave climbed into the saddle, put the horse to the upgrade and joined the other.

They rode north-west, down the far slopes of the foothills, riding side by side most of the time. Cressidy sat slouched forward in the saddle, his hat brim pulled well down over his eyes, shading out the glare of the sun. It was high noon now and already the heat was beginning to tell on men and beasts. Cressidy could have been asleep from the loose way he sat in the saddle, his body swaying easily with every movement of his mount. But he was not asleep and his eyes missed nothing.

Dave rode in silence. He made no further comment about the men at the ranch but, inwardly, his mind was racing, assessing the immediate possibilities and trying to formulate a plan in the light of this new and unexpected development.

By mid-afternoon they rode down the hills, on to the smooth grassy plain, through the gap in the twisted boundary fence and on to the ranch. From the subdued sounds he heard as they approached, it did not seem that there could be as many men there as Cressidy had intimated. Then he rode into full view of the place, saw the gaudily saddled horses milling around in the corral, knew that Marengo had been as good as his word, had bought his *vaqueros* along with him. He reined up in the dusty courtyard, swung down as several men appeared around the corner of the half-built shack, recognised Don Ricardo Marengo among them.

8

Gunsmoke Reckoning

There were few people about in the streets of Big Stone Gap when Clem Tollison rode in, carrying his son's body across the saddle of his horse. It was almost dark with the first stars just beginning to show in the east, the cool time of the evening, when most of the people were in their homes or inside the saloons. The tinny sound of a piano floated out from one of the saloons as the party of riders rode in silence towards the undertaker's. Reining up, Clem turned his head, spoke to two of his men.

'Take Jeb's body inside, boys, then meet me over at the saloon in half an hour. We've got some work to do tonight, something that isn't going to wait any longer.'

Jerking the reins around, he walked his mount across to the sheriff's office, got down and went inside, the brief glare of yellow light showing for an instant as he passed through the doorway. In the office, Ben Chapman looked up in surprise, then got heavily to his feet, staring at the rancher from across the desk. There was something on the older man's face that stopped the words of greeting that rose to his lips. Something had happened, something bad that boded ill for the town.

'I just brought Jeb into town,' Tollison said hollowly. 'I

discovered him shot in the chest out on the edge of the desert. There was no sign of his own Colt, but his rifle was lying some distance away.'

'You got any idea who did it?'

'I'm quite certain who it was. Dave Kelsey. Some of his friends broke him out of jail so that he wouldn't swing for murder. The first thing he did once he was free was lie in wait for my son and shoot him down without givin' him a chance to defend himself.'

'You want me to get a posse and ride out after Kelsey?'

'No need. I've brought my boys with me. There's to be no mistake this time. When I ride back into town, it will be Kelsey's dead body slung over the saddle.'

Chapman nodded. He moved around the front of the desk. 'By the way, Mister Tollison. There's somebody else in town I think you should have a talk with before you leave. He seems to have a similar interest in Dave Kelsey.'

'The guy you told me about?'

'Yes. Fellow by the name of Frenchy LaVere. He's got a room at the hotel. My guess is he's here to shoot it out with Kelsey as soon as they meet face to face.'

Tollison considered that for a moment, then moved towards the door. 'Reckon I should have a word with him,' he said, dryly.

The clerk behind the desk in the lobby of the hotel eyed Tollison in mild surprise as the other strode towards him. He got hesitantly to his feet. 'You lookin' for someone, Mister Tollison?' he stammered.

'That's right. Name of LaVere.'

'Front room at the end of the corridor at the top of the stairs.' The other pointed. 'You'll find him in. Doesn't usually go out at night. Just sits there after he finishes supper.'

He realised that he was speaking the last few words to himself. Tollison was already halfway up the stairs, his boots clattering on the creaking wood. The clerk stared after him for a moment, then went back to his seat and picked up his newspaper again, wondering briefly what business Clem Tollison might have with this stranger.

Tollison rapped loudly on the door at the end of the passage. For a moment there was no sound from the other side, then he heard the soft movement of a chair being scraped back, the shuffle of feet approaching and a voice asked: 'Yes, who is it?'

'My name is Tollison,' Clem said harshly. 'I want a word with you.'

There was a brief pause, then a key turned in the lock and the door opened. Tollison stepped inside as the other stood back, motioning him in. Closing the door, LaVere said: 'I sort of figured I might get a visit from you, Tollison. I think I know why you're here.'

'Perhaps. I've been hearin' things about you and I think the time has come to know why you're here. They say you're lookin' for Kelsey. Some sort of feud between the two of you?'

'Somehow, I think that's my business,' LaVere said. His tone was quiet, but there was an undertone of menace to it, giving it a faintly glacial quality, and Tollison's face stiffened as he turned and stared hard at the other.

'I'm afraid that you don't understand your position here in town,' he said, after a brief, appraising pause. 'I don't know what it is between you and Kelsey, but I have a score to settle with him and I aim to allow nothing to stand in my way. Kelsey has already killed two of my sons. For that I mean to kill him.'

'Then we both want the same thing,' LaVere said smoothly. He did not remove his cold stare from the other's face.

'Exactly. The question, however, is how do we intend to go about it? I know where Kelsey is at this very moment. I have more than forty men who will ride with me at half an hour's notice. Can you say the same?'

'No. But I have men here in town, just waitin' for me to give the order,' Frenchy said. He sat down in the chair near the small table, crossed his legs nonchalantly and lit a thin cheroot.

'How many men?' Tollison persisted.

'Enough for what I have in mind. I've been asking some discreet questions around town while I've been here. Seems that Kelsey doesn't have a friend in the world. He's a loner. Such a man is easy meat once he can be found. That is the only advantage he has. He can hide easily. But when his hiding place is known, he can die just as simply.'

Tollison shook his head. 'You've been gravely misinformed, my friend. Yesterday it would have been true to say that he had no friends. But that is no longer the case. My men have been watching all of the trails leading into and out of Big Stone Gap. They tell me that a large force of men rode in from the south and headed straight for the old Kelsey ranch.'

'What sort of men? Gunfighters?'

Tollison shrugged. 'That could be. They were Mexicans.'

'So.' Frenchy nodded his head slowly. He got to his feet and took a quick turn around the room, puffing on the cheroot. 'I must apologise, my friend. This I did not know. But I can see what has happened. Perhaps I am a fool for not having realised it before.'

'You know who these men are?'

'They are *vaqueros* riding with a man named Don Ricardo Marengo. It is with him, as well as with Kelsey, that I have a quarrel.'

'Then you can't hope to destroy Kelsey with the few men you have.'

Frenchy brooded a moment. He peered through the upcurl of smoke from the cheroot with narrowed eyes. 'So what do you suggest? I guess you have something in mind otherwise you would not have come here.'

'I don't see any reason why you and I should fight this out between ourselves. I want Kelsey dead. So do you. If we join forces, our chances of success are materially increased.'

LaVere reached his decision. 'Very well. When do you ride out?'

'In half an hour. Get your men together and meet us in front of the saloon.'

Three hours later, after an uneventful ride out from town, the tightly knit bunch of men reined up in the upper reaches of an arroyo to the east of the Kelsey spread. The atmosphere was heavy with tension. Tollison could feel it eating at his nerves as he stepped down from the saddle, walked to the edge of the deep cut and stared out into the darkness. There was a low moon, but as yet it came scarcely above the tops of the nearby trees and gave them little light. A battalion of tricky shadows moved over the sweeping plain that led all the way down to the burnt-out shell of the ranch.

'Is that the place?' LaVere asked tautly. He lifted his rifle from its scabbard.

'That's it,' Tollison nodded. 'We have to be careful now. They'll have posted guards to watch the trail. I don't want anyone to give the alarm until we're all in position.'

'Don't we have enough men between us to just rush the place?'

'Maybe we could at that,' said Tollison, with a touch of sarcasm in his tone. 'Very likely we'd eventually smash them down, but we'd lose most of our men in the attack.'

'So what's your plan?'

'We'll move in nice and easy, hit 'em from all sides before they're ready for us. If we can get 'em all bunched together like steers down there, we can pin 'em down without any real trouble. I figure they won't have any store of ammunition in that shack yonder.'

LaVere made as if to argue the point further, then closed his mouth with an audible snap, turned away to where his men stood in a small bunch. He did not like the idea too much. It held the promise of a long, drawn-out gun battle which was not to his liking. The desire to see both Kelsey and Marengo grovelling in the dirt in front of him was an unbearable ache in his body.

As darkness had settled, the *vaqueros* had moved into the wide courtyard. Marengo had posted three of them on the low heights overlooking the trail, and throughout the long hours of evening the men had sat in small huddled groups, talking among themselves in low whispers, waiting for something they knew would come sooner or later.

Grinding the stub of his cigarette into the dirt, Dave Kelsey glanced at Marengo out of the corner of his eye. The Mexican was seated near the wooden rail, sagging in places, which had once run along the front of the wide porch. He was busily cleaning his gun, easing the oil-soaked rag through it, wiping it carefully, almost lovingly. He glanced up as he felt the other's eyes on him.

'Have you ever had that feeling that there is trouble just about to break, *amigo*?' Marengo asked softly. 'That feeling you sometimes get when there is a thunderstorm breaking over the horizon, too far away to be felt, but near enough for some strange sense to warn you that it is there?'

'I know the kind of feeling you mean.'

'I have had it for over an hour now. It has been growing stronger every minute.'

'Tollison? You think he's headed this way?'

The other nodded. 'He will surely have had spies watching the trails. They will have seen my men and myself ride in here and reported back to him. That is the way they did it in the army, is it not? So he knows that, unless he strikes soon, everything is lost. Because once the townsfolk know we are here, they will seize their chance and join us.'

'I only wish I could be as sure of that as you are.' Dave sat in the dimness, listening to the wind rustling in the tall grass and murmuring around the thick wooden planks and beams. It would moan softly at first and then rise to a faintly shrieking sound, bringing sand with it, hurling the whirling grains against the wall of the shack behind him.

Sitting there, it kept going through his mind: 'What action would you take if you were Clem Tollison?'

It was impossible to answer that question. Tollison was the unknown quantity. He might do as Marengo had figured and ride against them that night, giving them no time to prepare. Or on the other hand, he might hold off for several days.

Ten o'clock came and went. Then eleven. The moon drifted clear of the horizon and the stars were tiny pinpoints of light. He stretched himself out with his legs straight in front of him, his back and shoulders resting against the wall. He could hear the snickers of the horses in the corral, an occasional murmur of conversation from some of the men, but in the main the night was quiet.

It must have been almost one o'clock and he had been dozing fitfully when the sound of the revolver shot shattered the stillness, and he heard a sharp yell from somewhere in the distance. The first thing he thought of was Tollison. Beside him Marengo rolled up on to one elbow, thrust himself to his feet, suddenly wide awake, grabbing for his rifle as he came upright.

'What is it?' Dave asked tautly.

The moon had drifted behind a bank of thick cloud and it was pitch dark so that he could see nothing with any degree of certainty. In the stillness that followed the racketing echoes of the gunshot, he heard a man nearby lever a shell into his rifle.

'One of the guards, up there on the hill yonder,' Marengo's tight whisper came to him from the blackness. 'He may have been shooting at shadows, but I doubt it.'

The silence grew long. Tension crackled in the faint breeze. It needed only the slightest movement or sound to start off the guns, but for what seemed an eternity there was nothing, so that after a pause Dave was beginning to feel that he had either imagined or dreamt the sound of that shot.

Then, without warning, all hell erupted around them.

Colts and rifles opened up in a vicious bedlam of sound.
Bullets hummed through the darkness and smashed into
the walls of the shack at their backs. Instinctively, Dave
flung himself down on to the hard ground, jerking the
Colt from its holster as he hit the dirt. He could see no
human target out there in the anonymous velvet blackness
of the night, but the brief stilettos of the muzzle flashes
pinpointed the positions of the enemy.

Firing swiftly, he ran forward, flung himself down
behind a pile of wood, lay there gasping air into his lungs
as the racket of answering fire from Marengo's men
crashed out all about him. The looming hills took up the
noise, seemed to magnify it out of all proportion and hurl
it back at him until his ears rang with it and the beating
roar hammered through his head.

A horse whinnied nearby. There was a faint insect-hum
close to his ear. Splinters of wood flew through the air
from where the bullet had struck and he felt something
thin and sharp embed itself in the fleshy part of his neck.
Reaching up instinctively, he pulled the sliver out, felt the
warmth of blood on his neck, trickling down from the
deep puncture.

A few moments later the moon sailed out into the open,
flooding the scene in front of him with a cold, eerie radiance. A multitude of shadows sprang into existence, each
one seemingly endowed with life and movement all its
own. His instinct was to fire at each one, but he restrained
himself with an effort of will. For some seconds he could
see nothing definite. Then he picked out a crashing in the
brush off to his right, turned his head and peered in the
direction of the ruined bunkhouse. A trio of dark figures
suddenly launched themselves into the open and raced
across the level stretch of ground, heads bent low, legs
pumping as hard as they could go. His first shot hit the
leading man, sent him sprawling face down in the dust. He
was dead before he hit the ground. The other two came
on recklessly. Taking a careful aim, he squeezed the trig-

ger again, saw one of the other men stumble, almost fall, catch his balance and stagger on, flopping out of sight some twenty yards away. His companion went down with him and both commenced firing at Dave.

Dave waited. It would have been sheer suicide to move while these two men were there, pinning him down, covering every move he made.

Lifting himself slowly, he sent three shots bracketing the spot where the two men had gone down. For a moment nothing happened. Then one of them threw himself forward, angling around the perimeter of the corral, bobbing and weaving from side to side, firing as he ran. Dave threw two shots at him, missed with both, cursed as he pulled down his head to reload the gun. Thumbing shells into the empty chambers, he listened to the shifting intensity of the gunfire, trying to gauge where the main enemy force lay. It was soon obvious that Tollison had deployed his men all the way around the place, determined to pin him down there.

There was a sudden movement beside him and Marengo dropped down into the dust behind the pile of wood. He said harshly: 'They have the place surrounded, *amigo*. I have the strange feeling that we are heavily outnumbered.'

Dave's eyes remained on the low ridge in the distance. If he knew Tollison, the other would not be risking his hide among the gunfighters. He would be back there somewhere, possibly with the horses, giving the orders.

'Cover me,' he hissed sharply. He checked his gun, then moved forward slowly.

'Don't be a goddamn fool,' said the other, divining his intention. 'You don't stand a chance.'

'Just cover me.' Dave ignored the other's protest. Getting his feet under him, he paused for just a few seconds, then ran forward. A couple of slugs ploughed into the dirt around his feet as he ran. Behind him, he heard the reassuring bark of the Mexican's rifle. As he drew level with the spot where the two men had gone down under cover, he paused, spotted the shadowy figure lying on the ground and automatically lowered the barrel of the Colt, finger tightening on the trigger. Then he relaxed the pressure. The man lay on his face, arms and legs outflung, and he did not move. Leaping over him, not giving him a second glance, Dave raced on. The roar of gunfire closed in around him now. Lunging and stumbling he reached the grass at the foot of the rise. From above him he could hear the harsh yells of the men crouched under cover and once he fancied he heard Tollison's harsh tones, but he could not be certain, and the voice was not repeated.

He could make out the ledge now as the clouds passed in front of, and then away from the face of the moon. The thudding blast of guns hammered at the air about him. It seemed incredible that Tollison had managed to get so many men together. Small wonder that he succeeded in ruling the surrounding territory with a hand of iron.

A man rushed towards Dave, looming up from the darkness. His head was thrust forward as he peered closely at him, lips drawn back across his teeth. Whether it was instinct or something more than that which warned him of his danger it was impossible to tell. But he opened his mouth wide to utter a loud, warning cry, went for his guns, clawing them free of leather as Dave fired.

The shot lifted the man up on to his toes, spun him half around. Gasping, he seemed to hang there for a long moment. Then he went down on to his face.

Crouching down, Dave heard the confused shouting around him. A shot came from the darkness and the slug burned along his arm, as if a red-hot poker had been suddenly laid on his flesh.

Moving into the trees, Dave faded into the tangled underbrush, the booming roar of the guns drowning the sound of his movement. He wanted to find the horses, guessing that there he might find Clem Tollison, possibly

Creede and Clem Junior if they had joined their father in this all out attempt to avenge the deaths of their brothers. The trees thinned, gave way to open spaces. Up ahead of him a horse snickered thinly. He felt the muscles of his stomach and chest tense. A few moments later he was able to make out the horses, all clustered together in a tight bunch, milling around in a clearing a little larger than the others.

At first he could see no one with them. Then, on the far side of the clearing, two figures detached themselves from the dark background of bushes and trees, moving towards him. Clem Tollison and Creede, shorter and more stockily built. They paused when they were still twenty feet away. Dave waited for only a moment, then pushed his way through the undergrowth, saw the two men look up sharply.

'That you, Frank?' called Clem sharply.

Abruptly, at the sound of the other's voice, the eruptive forces that had been a part of Dave's make-up for so long surged completely out of control.

'I'm goin' to give you both the chance you never gave my father,' he said in a soft, very soft voice. He thrust the gun back into its holster as he strode forward, pausing when he was less than ten feet away. 'I'm goin' to give you the chance to go for your guns before I shoot you down.'

'You!' said Clem. He seemed unable to believe his eyes. For a moment he did not move. Then he said softly: 'I'm sure you aren't such a fool as to think you could get as far as this without bein' covered. There are half a dozen rifles trained on you from the bushes at this very moment. And if you make one move towards your gun, you're a dead man. Far better if you were to call off your men.'

'Just keep talkin',' Dave said thinly. 'It doesn't make one bit of difference as far as you're concerned. If there were any rifles trained on me I'd have been dead by now, because that's the way you operate. Shoot men in the back before they have a chance to defend themselves and—'

The Proud Rebel

Before he had finished speaking, both men went for their guns. Dave hurled himself sideways and down, the Colt in his hand spitting flame and smoke while he was still in a horizontal position in mid-air. He saw Creede Tollison drop as a slug took him between the eyes. The older man was still on his feet although Dave's second bullet had taken him dead centre. But he was beginning to sway and weave as he fought desperately to keep the life in his eyes, fighting with every ounce of strength and determination in him, with every bit of tenacious venom, to stay on his feet and run this string out to its very end.

His lips were drawn hard back from his teeth, his grin a white gash in the shadow of his face, some dark and dreadful concentration showing in the deep-set eyes and the lines of his face as he struggled to focus every last atom in his body into the act of bringing up the gun for one last convulsive pressure on the trigger.

But even for a man like Clem Tollison, there had to be a limit to that kind of thing. Slowly his knees buckled under him as though unable to bear his weight any longer. He found it impossible to swing the heavy gun up into line. He could not even force the strength into his hand to pull the trigger. It was suddenly impossible for him even to breathe or see. All that he could do was topple forward on to his face and fall into a never-ending darkness that marked the end of his world, his life.

Dave walked forward very slowly with measured steps. The horses shied away from him, spooked a little by the scent of gunsmoke and death that eddied in the clearing. He turned both bodies over with his boot. He needed no closer examination. Both men were dead.

Edging away from the clearing, he moved nearer to the trees. There was a strange emptiness in him now that part of the chore was finished and done with. Even the racket of gunfire failed to rouse him. Reaching the long piece of rope that had been stretched between the trunks of two trees, with the reins of the horses hitched along it, he untied the knot from one end, then fired a single shot into the air. The frightened animals lunged forward, swung off across the clearing, thundering into the night. At least none of the gunmen still on their feet would ride out of there.

He turned to move back through the trees, then stopped short in his tracks as a voice he recognised at once said: 'Hold it right there, Kelsey.'

Dave twisted his head slowly. Frenchy LaVere stood just inside the rim of trees. There was an evil grin twisting his face and the moonlight, striking in a net through that close-packed tangle of branches overhead, glinted off the gun in his right hand.

'I figured you might try something like this if you got half a chance, so I decided to wait for you. The shoe is on the other foot this time. I swore in Clayton that I would even the score. I reckon that this is the time to do it.'

Standing helplessly in the middle of the clearing, Dave knew with a sick certainty that he could not hope to draw and shoot before LaVere pressed the trigger that would send a slug speeding into his body. But since there was no other choice left open to him, his right hand flashed towards the gun butt and, in the same instant, he threw himself down and sideways. LaVere's weapon roared. Dave felt himself driven forward as the lead took him in the shoulder, high up, the sharp shock of the bullet hammering into the muscles. He staggered, felt himself falling forward even as, by some sheer effort of will, he twisted around, bringing up his right hand in a purely reflex movement. There seemed to be only sufficient strength in his finger for one shot. The bullet went wide, slicing a piece of bark from one of the trees a foot or more from where Frenchy stood. The other's grin widened. Slowly and painfully, Dave rolled over on to his good side, his hand trying to lift the gun once more. But it seemed suddenly to have gained a tremendous weight which it had never possessed before. Eyes blurring, the waves of agony washing through him in time to the pounding beat of his heart, he watched as the other lifted his gun again, taking a couple of steps forward. It would be impossible for him to miss this time.

'This way, LaVere!'

With a wrench of his neck muscles, Dave turned his head. The shadowy figure standing just inside the trees was only dimly recognisable as Ricardo Marengo. There was no doubt that the Mexican could have killed the other where he stood without warning, but some sense of fairness had prompted him to call the other's name.

Frenchy swung sharply. His right hand was a blur of speed as he levelled the gun and fired in the same fluid movement. Both guns seemed to go off at the same moment, the shots blurring into each other. Lying there, Dave saw Marengo flinch, saw his left arm jerk as the bullet tore into it, smashing the wrist.

Then he switched his glance back to LaVere. The gambler was teetering on his feet, swaying drunkenly, arms hanging by his sides. His face was a grey blur in the moonlight, teeth showing faintly in a grimace of vague disbelief. Then all of the life seemed to die from his eyes. He went down on to his knees, hung there for several seconds, before he fell forward.

Gritting his teeth, fighting desperately against the weakness that threatened to overwhelm him completely, Dave staggered to his feet. He could feel the blood oozing down his back, his shirt sticking to the flesh. Marengo came forward. He looked about him. The three bodies lay still and silent in the clearing.

Softly he said: 'It is all over as far as they are concerned, *amigo*. But you have been badly hurt.'

'Nothing. Just a bit of lead in my shoulder. Probably looks a lot worse than it is.'

Dave made to follow the other, tried to say something more, but the words were scarcely a mutter. A wavering darkness seemed to be dimming his eyes and he felt himself slipping forward into an all-enveloping blackness that was strangely devoid of any pain.

When he eventually drifted back to consciousness, he found himself in familiar and yet unfamiliar surroundings. He tried to lift his head, but the throbbing, pounding ache soon made him desist and he let it fall back on to the soft pillow. Only several minutes later did recognition come to him. This was the room he had slept in that night he had ridden up to Stacy's back door. Yet how could he have possibly got here? For a second he had the dread feeling that it was a delirium, a product of a fevered brain. Then he heard the door open and soft footsteps approached the bed. Forcing his eyes to remain open, he looked up.

'So you're finally awake,' said Stacy. 'You know you gave us all quite a scare when they brought you in. You've been delirious for about two days. How are you feeling now?'

'Two days?' Dave screwed up his forehead as he struggled to comprehend. 'But I—'

Stacy placed a finger on his lips. 'The doctor says you mustn't try to talk or excite yourself. He'll drop by and take another look at you this afternoon. In the meantime, you've to lie here and remain quiet.'

'What happened, Stacy? Out at the ranch, I mean.'

For a moment there was a serious expression on her face. Then she said in a low tone: 'Clem and Creede Tollison are dead. Clem Junior pulled up stakes and left town yesterday. Nobody knows where he went and nobody really cares. Frenchy LaVere is dead, too. I'd say that all of Tollison's men, those who survived the gunfight, have been scattered. They won't come back and cause any further trouble. They are men who only fight for those who pay the most for their guns.'

'And Ricardo?'

'Alive and kicking. There's no call to worry about him,' Stacy smiled warmly at him. 'Well, you'd better get some rest while I make you something to eat. There'll be plenty of time for you to start asking questions when you feel stronger.'

She turned and went out of the room. Dave lay there, staring up at the ceiling, turning over his thoughts in his mind. Was it possible that it was all over, that here he had the chance to make a new, fresh start? It was as if a tremendous weight had suddenly been lifted off his mind. He waited impatiently for Stacy to come back. There were several very important questions that he had to ask her....

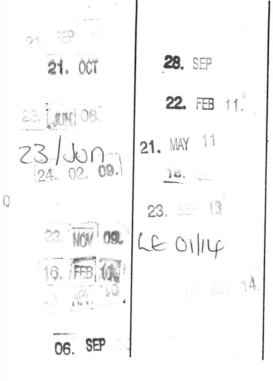

21. SEP

21. OCT

28. SEP

22. FEB 11.

21. MAY 11

23. JUN 08.

23/Jun

24. 02. 09.

18.

23. SEP 13

LE 01/14

0

23. NOV 09.

16. FEB 1

APF

NOV 14.

06. SEP

Rhif/No. _____ Dosb./Class _____

Dylid dychwelyd neu adnewyddu'r eitem erbyn neu cyn y dyddiad a nodir uchod.
Oni wneir hyn gellir codi tal.

This book is to be returned or renewed on or before the last date stamped above,
otherwise a charge may be made.

LLT1